'You're wrong!' Verity countered, suppressing her temper. 'I did love Edward!'

'No. You did not love Edward. If you had, you would never have responded to me the way you did that night in Florida,' Luc asserted quietly.

'Luc, that's a *foul* thing to suggest! And you're a fine one to talk about love! What about the way you treated your wife?' she said in a choked voice.

Dear Reader

We are always keen at Mills & Boon to discover more about our readers' likes and dislikes. This month, we want to know what you think about our heroes! He is always in command and always a real catch, but do you like your hero to be just that little bit on the side of dangerous—ruthless even? Or do you like him to be gentle and caring, and unashamed to show it?

Do you like a gentleman or a rake? And what about foreign heroes? We'd love to know so put pen to paper and tell us.

The Editor

Having abandoned her first intended career for marriage, **Rosalie Ash** spent several years as a bilingual Personal Assistant to the Managing Director of a leisure group. She now lives in Warwickshire with her husband, and daughters Kate and Abby, and her lifelong enjoyment of writing has led to her career as a novelist. Her interests include languages, travel and research for her books, reading, and visits to the Royal Shakespeare Theatre in nearby Stratford upon Avon. Other pleasures include swimming, yoga and country walks.

Recent titles by the same author:

LOVE BY DESIGN
LAW OF THE CIRCLE

THE WITCH'S WEDDING

BY
ROSALIE ASH

MILLS & BOON LIMITED
ETON HOUSE   18-24 PARADISE ROAD
RICHMOND   SURREY   TW9 1SR

*First published in Great Britain 1992
by Mills & Boon Limited*

© Rosalie Ash 1992

*Australian copyright 1992
Philippine copyright 1992
This edition 1992*

ISBN 0 263 77761 8

*Set in Times Roman 10 on 12 pt.
01-9210-54286 C*

Made and printed in Great Britain

CHAPTER ONE

THE first letter arrived on Monday morning, while Verity was eating toast and ginger marmalade for breakfast. The Florida postmark made her heart jolt without warning. Florida. Luc was playing polo in Florida. It had to be from Luc. She stared thoughtfully at her address, written in heavy black ink on the blue envelope.

How unusual to get a letter from him. Luc hardly ever wrote to her. They'd spoken on the phone last week, their usual brief, cool, businesslike exchange, about some friends of his who needed a caterer for their niece's eighteenth birthday party. He'd been vague about the details. Could he have written to her about it, with more information...?

Finally she abandoned her pointless conjectures and ripped it open. With annoyingly unsteady hands, she withdrew a sheet of blue airmail paper and began to read the broad, scrawling black script until she let out a yelp of surprised protest which brought Sara dashing from the bathroom.

'What's wrong? Bad news?'

Verity shook her head slowly, eyes wide with disbelief.

'No... surprising, that's all... but Luc's mad. Totally insane. I can't possibly...'

Sara gave an impatient exclamation and began reading over Verity's shoulder.

'... two weeks' *working* holiday in the Dominican Republic, all expenses paid...' she read aloud incredu-

5

lously. 'I like the "working" part! And where on earth is the Dominican Republic, if you please?'

'I'm not sure!' Verity laughed doubtfully, shaking her mane of hazel-gold curls jerkily back from her face. 'Somewhere in the Caribbean, I think. Luc must have sunstroke or something!'

'Are you sure it isn't a joke?' Sara was frowning over the rest of the letter. 'You know what a warped sense of humour the man has.'

Verity read the letter again. It was typical of Luc's style of speech, brief and slightly cryptic. Further details would follow. He advised her to get malaria, typhoid and hepatitis jabs. Fairly quickly, as her flight was booked for Friday the tenth of April. He assured her the accommodation had his personal recommendation, and he knew Sara could cope for a couple of weeks. And since he had friends who needed an experienced caterer to organise a series of house-parties at their holiday villa, Verity could combine a fortnight in the sun with some lucrative business...

'It isn't a joke,' Sara confirmed happily, as Verity turned to stare at her, a stunned expression in her pansy-brown eyes.

'No...'

There was a silence which stretched for several seconds. Then Sara frowned teasingly at Verity's anxious face.

'Verity, darling, you look as if you've just opened the gas bill instead of a wonderful offer of a Caribbean holiday from our chief patron and mentor! If I had a friend like Luc García I'd be dancing around the flat in ecstasy right now!'

'Sara, that's just it...I mean, Luc's been very...*kind*, and helpful since Edward died but...but I couldn't describe us as *friends*! I hardly ever see him...'

Mainly through choice, she had to admit, with a twist of bitter memory. Since the fiasco of their first meeting, and the ghastly trauma immediately following it, she'd deliberately avoided too much personal contact with Luc García. An evasion he seemed bent on making as difficult as possible for her, with all his contacts and recommendations for her catering business, most of them undetectable until some chance remark threw Luc's name yet again into the proceedings...

A mental picture of Luc's craggy dark face and electric-blue eyes swam briefly into her mind, and she frowned even harder. Bearing in mind that she hardly ever saw him, and that he was one of her least favourite people on this planet, it was unnerving how clearly she could conjure his image. Equally unnerving was the way the mere memory of his forceful personality could send a *frisson* of awareness slithering down her spine. Anger and self-contempt struggled for supremacy, and she gritted her teeth, fighting for calm.

'I just cannot imagine why he's dreamed this up!' she went on defensively. 'There must be dozens and dozens of caterers in this Dominican Republic...'

'But none he can personally recommend?' Sara finished up reasonably, shaking her short blonde hair out of her eyes.

Verity's insides were doing a series of acrobatics that made her feel slightly sick. She had no idea how she should react to such an offer. Luc's unavoidable generosity over the last twelve months was one thing, but *this* proposition was so sudden, so totally unexpected...but, on the other hand, it was also a business opportunity, wasn't it? And if she could bear to be honest with herself, the success so far of her business was mainly due to Luc García's recommendations and contacts, wasn't it...? Was it right to hold a grudge this long, and after all these subtle 'olive-branches' extended over the last twelve months?

She sighed, turning to gaze unseeingly out of the window. It was a question of trust, she decided bleakly. And trust wasn't an emotion she could ever link with Luc García, thinking about their first meeting, almost exactly a year ago.

He was to have been best man at her wedding to Edward. But, just a week after she'd been introduced to Luc, Edward had broken his neck on the polo field, falling from his horse at high speed.

Verity winced as the thoughts crowded back, unbidden. That terrible day, when she'd watched Edward killed, would always be with her. But so, in a completely different way, would that first meeting with Luc...

It always gave her a dismayed jolt to admit the strange impact of that meeting with Edward's friend and 'hero'. The moment was still so vivid, she could almost feel the Florida sun that March day, smell the pungent blend of horses and sweat and adrenalin and expensive perfume in the air, which seemed to typify polo matches wherever the venue.

Not that she'd been to that many. The leisured life and freedom to flit between social events had seemed an unlikely luxury, since she'd always had to earn her own living. Linking some form of lucrative work to anything else she undertook had been a necessity. Even her holidays were always working holidays. She'd met Edward the previous season, while she was just nineteen and employed as a chalet girl in the Val-d'Isère, getting invaluable experience of catering for house-parties. Edward, who'd loved skiing as well as polo, had arrived with a large group of friends, and their relationship had blossomed during that fortnight.

Fiercely independent, she'd only agreed to join him while he played polo in Florida last March after getting a temporary job as cook to some friends of Edward's parents. At that time she'd been struggling to establish her own business, with limited success. People always said it wasn't what you knew, but who you knew. She'd wryly discovered the truth of this saying, as she battled with stern competition from a host of other young women with similar aspirations but more useful connections. Coming from an obscure boarding convent in the west country held little sway against girls from top Swiss finishing schools with relatives in all the right places.

Verity took a calmly philosophical view, and stubbornly resolved to succeed through her own abilities. She didn't need wealthy, aristocratic contacts. All she needed was 'word of mouth' approval, by people who'd experienced her cooking talents at first hand...

That day last March, as the polo match finished and the players rode, dusty and triumphant, from the field, Edward, his blond hair glinting flaxen in the sun, his grey eyes alight with the boyish laughter she'd always found so endearing, had introduced her to Luc with a sort of joky reverence. But she hadn't needed to be told this particular player's name. She'd heard his reputation, and found her eyes reluctantly fixed on him throughout the match.

Even at a distance he had magnetism. Her gaze was drawn and held almost hypnotically by the savagely ef-

fective technique of the team's much-fêted high-goal
South American patron.

Close up, the brilliant electric-blue of that lidded gaze,
contrasting with the swarthy darkness of his skin, was
unforgettable. As if she had an indelible picture in her
head, she could remember every detail of his appearance
as he jumped down from a sweating dark bay horse.
Dusty white breeches, white gloves, blue polo shirt, blue
hard hat, long tan leather boots, leather belt, knee pads,
straps and spurs . . . every trivial detail had somehow im-
printed itself on her reluctant subconscious.

With the light breeze blowing the full skirt of her floral
silk dress against her legs, and teasing the gold strands
of her topknot from their secure fastening, she'd stood
there, transfixed, attempting a politely unconcerned smile
but just for a few seconds lost in that dark-lashed blue
gaze.

A hard brown hand had grasped her own in greeting,
with a brief, swift appraisal. Then he'd retained it for
just a fraction of a second longer than courtesy decreed.
It was as if he'd sensed her awareness, and was casually
probing for more information, with that wordless body
language that was a hallmark of his arrogance . . .

And if she'd found him unnervingly attractive, she
hadn't been alone, she reflected drily. Scores of pairs of
female eyes appeared to be trained permanently on Luc
García. On the bar terrace afterwards, women swarmed
around him like bees round a honeypot. When she'd
laughingly commented on it to Edward, he'd made a
wry face and nodded.

'Women like Luc, and Luc likes women, plural,' he'd
agreed, giving her a quick hug and dropping a possessive kiss on her mouth. 'Not like me. There's only
one girl for me . . .'

But Edward's voice had held a note of admiration for Luc, even so. And Verity's stifled feeling of indignation at that moment had been nothing compared with the shock of fury and humiliation she experienced, dancing with Luc at the club ball that night, and bumping into him alone, later still on the moonlit terrace...

'Verity? You're staring into space like a zombie, darling! Did you hear what I said?'

Sara was looking commendably patient.

'No, sorry. What did you say?'

'I said, Luc's obviously doing it because he knows how you might be feeling right now,' she said slowly, as if she were reasoning it out for a small child. 'Forget the macho beef-cake image—he's sensitive enough to guess you're depressed, almost exactly twelve months after Edward died.'

'But why would he feel it necessary to go to this length to cheer me up?' Verity demanded rather wildly, standing up and staring at the letter in confusion. Sara's choice of words had struck home. She didn't feel depressed, exactly... she felt guilty, just as she'd always felt guilty, ever since Edward died. Sometimes, at her lowest ebb, she had the notion that Edward's death had been some sort of fearful punishment for lacking the courage to face up to her true feelings.

And somehow Luc García always seemed to boost that guilt to an unbearable level, for reasons she found too painful to analyse...

'Over the past twelve months Luc's increased my volume of business by about three hundred per cent as it is!' she finished up with illogical resentment. 'I feel sufficiently indebted to the wretched man to last me a lifetime!'

Sara raised her eyebrows in mild mockery.

'Are you, by any chance, trying to tell me you're refusing this wonderful offer of a free holiday, with a spot of work thrown in for good measure, Verity, darling?'

Verity dragged her fingers through her hair, and then chewed distractedly on her thumbnail, before remembering a New Year's resolution and thrusting her hand into the pocket of her cinnamon-coloured bathrobe.

'I don't know! I just don't know what... what construction to put on it. Why *would* he do something like this?'

'Who knows?' Sara laughed, exasperated. 'Maybe it's meant to be a surprise birthday present! It is your birthday on the eleventh, isn't it? So, since he's paying, I'd just say thanks very much, and make the most of it if I were you!'

'But I can't—it seems so unfair on you, left holding the fort...'

'Nonsense. Verity Lacey Catering was your brainchild. You started up the business in the first place. You deserve the glamorous bits. Fair's fair.'

'Yes, but...'

'But nothing! We're a partnership, remember? I take holidays too. I might try and take some time off later in the year to see my brother and his new baby in Australia, if funds allow, that is! And since you've virtually just admitted that Luc's got the business up and running for us, quite frankly this isn't the time to get on the wrong side of him, is it?'

'Sara, don't be so mercenary!' Verity protested, with a slight laugh, but a cold feeling was creeping up her spine. Surely Sara wasn't suggesting that Luc might *damage* their business in some way if she didn't jump when he pulled the strings? That was her own melodramatic paranoia taking over!

'It's not mercenary, it's practical,' Sara asserted, blithely pouring herself a fresh cup of black coffee from the *cafetière*. 'Luc passes no end of business our way. Thanks to him, turnover is up and profits are rising. I can see the light at the end of a long dark tunnel, and so can you!'

'Yes, I know, but...'

'Any way you look at it, it makes solid business sense to humour the man! With his influence in high places, if he says you should spend two weeks working for him in some sunny spot, you should damn well do as he says!'

'You think so?' Verity's smile was wry, as she hid her deep misgivings. Did Luc García really command such unquestioning obedience? And if that was the case, why had she always had such an overpowering urge to run and hide from the man?

'I know so.' Sara was blithely determined. 'I'm *green* with envy, but you've had a rough twelve months, Verity, love. You deserve a break. Just don't lie around getting a golden tan to come back and taunt me with!'

Verity looked down blankly at the letter in her hands, quite unable to sort out her feelings. A fortnight in the Caribbean. All organised without her knowledge in a high-handed manner which was typical of Luc García. Should she swallow her pride, be mature and forgiving, bury the past, feel flattered that he thought so highly of her abilities, and accept? Or thank him politely, but tell him she had far too much work here in England to leave Sara to cope alone?

And the flight was booked for Friday the tenth—that was in about ten days' time. Even if she opted to go, could she possibly organise everything by then? Clothes, tickets, passport, injections...?

'Further details to follow,' she read aloud, almost to herself. 'Presumably that means tickets? Exact destination? Or do you think he intends a complete mystery tour?'

'I doubt it.' Sara laughed again, eyeing Verity's pole-axed expression with affection. 'Verity, darling, do wipe that "little girl lost" look off your face! All you have to do is go along to the doctor and get your injections, have a lot of fun buying ridiculous summer-holiday clothes in this month's sales, wait for your tickets to arrive, and get on a plane. Luc's not instructing you to cross the Atlantic single-handed in a bath-tub or anything. Stop looking so helpless!'

Verity put the letter down and expelled her breath slowly, turning to head for the bathroom. Sara was a very dear friend. An old schoolfriend from their boarding convent days. They went back a long way. Since she'd joined Verity as a business partner and joint owner of this spacious Victorian flat in Wimbledon, their relationship had gone from strength to strength. But even so, she'd never found herself able to confide in Sara about that deeply upsetting episode with Luc García, a year ago...

But she glanced back with a grateful grin, conscious, now more than ever, of how much she appreciated her friend's irrepressible good humour.

'Thanks, Sara... but I'm going to have to think very hard about this. I'm not at all sure whether it's a good idea...'

Verity thought about it constantly for the rest of the day, as, clad in jeans and sweatshirt, she set about transforming a huge, rather draughty Regency dining-room in Knightsbridge into a fairy-tale setting for a memorable meal. She loved her job. In that respect she supposed she was very lucky indeed, but not even her favourite occupation could drive away the turmoil of indecision over Luc's letter.

She paused at last to cast a critical eye over the results of her labours, assessing the gleaming froth of white gypsophila and cream and gold rosebuds adorning the long mahogany table and the chimney-piece. Her client was throwing a dinner party for twenty people, and in a few hours' time the table would be laden with rich food and expensive wine, and the room would be reverberating with the buzz of conversation and the chink of silver on bone china. There were tall cream scented candles in triple-branched silver candelabra placed strategically around the room. She itched to light the candles now. It was one of her small winter pleasures, lighting candles. A sort of symbolic gesture to the gods of light and warmth and survival.

The March evening outside was bleak and leafless, despite the rapid approach of spring, a forbidding grey and white landscape. An icy wind was keeping the temperatures well below zero. A vision of blue Caribbean skies, swaying green palms and hot sunshine swam into her mind, unbidden, and she slowly stretched out a slender, long-fingered hand to coax a creamy rosebud back into place in its silver bowl, re-examining her feelings about being indebted to Luc García.

Surely Sara was right? Wasn't she being ridiculously suspicious? Could she really let her private guilt feelings over the past colour her judgement over Luc's perfectly straightforward offer? Wouldn't she be mad to reject the chance of a fortnight in the sun just on some remembered grievance, and a foolish, buried fear about her feelings towards him? After all, it wasn't as if they even moved in the same world. Luc's globe-trotting life-

style, his exploits with a succession of glamorous women
constantly reported in the tabloid gossip pages—she and
Luc were so far removed from each other, they might
as well occupy different universes...so why worry about
briefly crossing paths with him again?

He wouldn't even *be* there, now she came to think
about it. He was a professional polo player. He'd be in
either Florida, or Argentina, where professional polo
players seemed prone to congregate at this time of year.
The only contact they'd have would be on the telephone,
with Luc relaying instructions through to wherever he'd
booked her in to stay...

By the time the second letter fell through the letter-
box the following morning, containing a fat wallet of
tickets and luggage labels from the travel agents, and
every kind of travel and health insurance it seemed
possible to organise, the whole prospect seemed to take
on a new reality. And, after a good night's sleep, the
pitfalls seemed less obvious, the advantages glaringly
apparent. Two weeks in the sun, away from the de-
pressing grey of England's skies, and profitable business
into the bargain.

Plus the chance to subtly convey to Luc that she'd
matured and gained in self-confidence, that he meant
nothing to her, never had and never would... She'd be
crazy to refuse...

Verity was catapulted out of her vagueness, and embarked on frenetic preparations. The hectic spell was
exaggerated by her determination to cook and freeze as
many exotic creations as she could to help Sara to cope
with her solo fortnight. There was also a mountain of
telephone and paperwork to bring rapidly up to date,
invoices and statements to check, but somehow, by the
night before she was due to leave, it was all done, and

she and Sara were thrusting her new tropical clothes into her suitcase, with Sara purring approvingly over each item.

'I *adore* this gold bikini, you know!'

'You should—you made me buy it!' Verity grinned, thrusting the lamentably minuscule garment firmly into the case beneath a pair of white drill Bermudas. 'At least you won't be around to bully me into actually *wearing* it!'

'I shall insist on photographic evidence to the affirmative!' Sara stated calmly, inspecting a gossamer-fine knee-length evening dress printed with apricot and gold roses, tiny gold shoe-string straps the only support on the low-cut bodice. 'This one is lovely, isn't it? Exactly your colouring. It'll look marvellous with a tan, and those gold leather thongy-things you bought.'

The thongy-things in question were fragile strappy sandals with slender high heels.

'Hardly suitable for solitary evening beach walks,' Verity had protested, as Sara nagged her into buying them.

'No, but ideal for dancing under velvet Caribbean skies with some dishy tall dark stranger you might meet!'

'Give my love-life a rest, Sara!' Verity had exclaimed laughingly. 'I'm going to be working, remember?'

'But not *all* the time! And won't the gorgeous Luc García be around?'

'Of course not, he's playing polo, remember? Presumably he'll ring me with the details of these house-parties, but he'll be hundreds of miles away! And as for not working all the time, I intend to earn my keep! Otherwise I'll feel too embarrassed, as if I'm accepting Luc's charity!'

Verity packed the last items—a swirly ankle-length cotton skirt in fine cream lawn, with a matching loose crop-top—before firmly shutting the case. 'Now you're quite sure you can cope...'

'Don't start all *that* again!' Sara gave her a quick hug. 'One more suggestion that I can't cope, and I shall take it as a direct insult. Have a wonderful time...'

Verity stiffened, suddenly reminded of something.

'Oh, lord, Sara! Tomorrow night! I was supposed to be seeing Elliot! I forgot all about it!'

Sara had gone very still at the mention of Elliot, and a slight flush crept into her cheeks.

'It's hardly the end of the world, is it?' she said finally, deceptively lightly. 'You *said* there was nothing serious between you...'

'There isn't... we're just friends!' Verity blurted out hastily. 'I mean I do *like* him, but not in that way... in fact, I'm sure he's desperately in love with someone else and doesn't know it yet...!'

Sara's green eyes clouded and her blush grew even deeper, suffusing her thin, elfin face, and Verity nibbled her thumb in vexation, wincing inwardly at her own sledge-hammer diplomacy, aware of a sudden tension in the air between them. It was a feeling she'd experienced before, whenever Elliot Grosvenor's name cropped up between Sara and herself.

Elliot was the brother of one of their regular clients, a blond, rather self-opinionated and incredibly rich City futures dealer who had apparently triggered love at first sight in Sara, but who'd made a perverse play for Verity ever since she'd made it patently obvious she wasn't interested. Verity had surreptitiously done her level best to push Elliot and Sara together, but only succeeded in getting herself in deeper than she'd intended. Elliot had pestered and pestered until she'd finally agreed to have dinner with him. But Friday's dinner date was to have been her last determined attempt at convincing Elliot he was pestering the wrong girl, without embarrassing Sara by revealing her feelings...

'I just don't like letting people down, that's all...' she finished up rather awkwardly.

'Do you want me to ring him for you?'

Verity hid a smile, and nodded enthusiastically.

'*Could* you, Sara, darling? Would that seem terribly rude, do you think?'

'I'll be the soul of discretion,' Sara promised quietly, turning away, but not before Verity had glimpsed the slight spark of anticipation in her friend's eyes.

She'd manoeuvre those two together if it was the last thing she did, Verity resolved firmly, as she progressed through the varying rituals of taxis, airports and aeroplanes the next day. Elliot was a complete idiot if he couldn't see what was staring him in the face...

Although being manoeuvred was a feeling niggling at the back of her own mind today. It wasn't that she was being manoeuvred in an unpleasant sense. You couldn't call having a surprise like this sprung on you unpleasant. It was just that she had a sensation, temporarily, as if her life was being neatly organised by others. In the kindest, most thoughtful way, of course. Leaving her feeling vaguely like a leaf in the wind, fluttering around with no control over her actions.

Sit back and enjoy it, a voice of wisdom told her silently. After two weeks in the sun, her normal calm, stubborn good humour would be well and truly restored. It must be healthy to relinquish control occasionally...

It was a pity, though, she decided, sitting in the Pan-Am jet as it soared along on its nine-hour flight to Miami, that, while the abstract concept of travelling was so exciting, the realities and mechanics of it were just the opposite.

She occupied her time reading a new historical romance she'd bought at the airport, dozing, and anticipating the exciting new recipes she'd be able to discover. The Dominican Republic should be bursting with exotic fruits and vegetables. She couldn't wait to explore the local markets, experiment with the local dishes. With luck, she'd bring a new Caribbean repertoire back to England with her in a fortnight's time...

In Miami, because of the time-difference, it was still only mid-afternoon. But by the time the connection across to the Dominican Republic was completed, via the stop-off in Port au Prince, it was getting on for ten o'clock at night, Caribbean time.

Staggering finally through Custom control, hot and tired, her cream gaberdine shirt-dress clinging uncomfortably in the tropical warmth, she was about to search out a taxi when she stopped abruptly in her tracks.

Her heavy leather suitcase still in her hand, she stared disbelievingly at the tall, hard-muscled man lounging against a black, open-top jeep, thick dark hair flopping in the familiar wedge over his forehead.

'Luc!' She felt glued to the spot. Somehow nothing, in the roller-coaster of events so far, had prepared her for the shock of seeing Luc García in person, waiting to meet her off the plane, a very relaxed, casual-looking Luc in faded denim Bermudas and white T-shirt, who threatened to dangerously rock her normal self-possession.

'You look as if you've seen a ghost,' he told her wryly, levering himself off the jeep and coming to take her case.

'I wasn't expecting to see you here...I...I mean, I thought you were playing polo!'

'I should be playing polo. In Argentina,' he agreed coolly. 'But I decided to take a little time off, en route from Florida.'

The electric brilliance of the blue gaze was, as usual, curiously hard to read but devastatingly destructive to her self-control.

'I wanted to make sure you turned up!' he added, with a shadow of a grin, gently prising her case from her nerveless fingers, and tossing it into the jeep.

The blue gaze was taking in every inch of her appearance, making her so self-conscious that she felt more sixteen than twenty-two, and, almost mesmerised, she found herself staring back at him as if she was seeing him properly for the first time.

Which was silly, she told herself sternly, because Luc had the kind of physical magnetism it was impossible to overlook. An odd collection of separate features which combined to make up a compelling whole, from his deepset, watchful, penetrating eyes to his long, slightly crooked nose, down to his wide, beautifully shaped, rather quirky mouth. A twist of humour deepened the lines which ran vertically from his nose to the outer corners of his mouth.

Recalling her resolutions when she decided to accept Luc's invitation, Verity took firm control of her wayward emotions.

'You mentioned a catering job,' she said with a cool laugh. 'Did you think I'd let you down?'

He shook his head, opening the passenger-door for her and moving around the vehicle with pantherish grace to swing in beside her. 'You're far too professional. But I'll admit it was short notice.'

'True. And incidentally, for future reference, the Caribbean is a little wide of my normal operating area,' she added with a half-smile.

'I thought you might like a change of scene.'

'Yes...that was very thoughtful of you.' She cast around for a neutral topic, his nearness in the cramped interior of the jeep playing havoc with her composure. 'How are you? How's the polo going?'

'OK. I'm still winning. How's business?'

'Business is very good...' She glanced at his strong profile as they began to drive. The dark night air, rushing past them as they followed a twisting road through armies of palm trees, was warm, spice-scented, filled with the high-pitched shrill of cicadas.

'Mainly thanks to you, I'm finding time to indulge myself with designing table and room settings as well as providing food!' she went on doggedly, striving for that calm maturity which implied she'd forgotten all about any past differences. 'In fact, I'm enjoying the artistic side almost as much as the cooking side...'

She hesitated, aware that the desired cool maturity was in danger of becoming a nervous gabble.

'But, while I love my job, I'm beginning to feel uncomfortably in your debt, Señor García!' she added, on a crisper note. 'And this surprise assignment you've conjured up for me here does nothing to lessen that feeling!'

Luc flashed her a glance in the darkness.

'Why?' He sounded grimly amused. 'I've got a gruelling schedule lined up for you. You'll be rushed off your feet.'

She wasn't sure how to interpret his tone.

'That's no problem; I love my job, as I said. And, with all my expenses paid for the trip out here, a gruelling schedule's the least I'd expect. I can't wait to start! So... what's the itinerary?'

There was a longish silence.

'Let me see,' Luc said finally, his tone expressionless. 'Tomorrow you're going to work very hard on your suntan, lying on the beach, sipping Ron Sours by the pool and sampling the local *mariscos*. The next few days, in fact the next couple of weeks, more of the same, plus maybe a little snorkelling around the coral reef, depending on the time available...'

Verity swung round in her seat to stare at him, a prickle of incredulous embarrassment rising up her neck and warming her cheeks.

'What about the catering you mentioned?' she queried, striving for calm. 'Surely I'll have to break off from this idyllic scenario once or twice to organise all these house-parties for your friends?'

Luc pulled off the road, and drew up outside the entrance to a long white building, Spanish-style, with archways, and a forest of tall dark coconut palms leaning at drunken angles all around it. Lights spilled from the doors and windows, picking out a crescent of silver beach and the dark swell of the sea.

'Only briefly, I'm afraid,' he told her gravely, turning to face her with mockery lurking in his narrowed blue gaze. 'My friends had to curtail their plans unexpectedly. There's only one party I'd like you to supervise. Towards the end of the second week. Just a small one...'

'*What*?' she burst out incredulously. 'You've got me out here *today*, and the only catering job you want me for is in two weeks' time? Luc, is this some sort of joke?'

He eyed her dispassionately for a few seconds, the brilliance of his gaze briefly driving all coherent thought from her mind.

'Not at all. For the past year you've worked every hour God sends,' he said blandly. 'Why are you so afraid to relax, Verity?'

'I happen to *like* working!' Verity pointed out with a crispness she was far from feeling. 'And if you think I'm going to accept your... your *charity*, lie around on the beach for two weeks at your expense...this *is* a joke, isn't it?'

'It's no joke.' Luc's voice held a disturbingly implacable note as he climbed out of the jeep. 'Edward died just over a year ago...'

'Do you think I've *forgotten* that?' she said in a low, shaky voice, fists clenched in angry frustration.

'And tomorrow is your birthday,' Luc went on, seemingly oblivious to her distress. 'I owe it to Edward to check that you're OK, twelve months on. Consider it a debt of honour, Verity. Enjoy yourself for two weeks. Charge it to my account.'

He paused to stare down at her in the darkness, a ruthless glint in his eyes. Verity swallowed on a dry throat, and lifted her chin defiantly.

'A debt of honour?' she echoed disbelievingly, her heart thudding against her ribcage. 'Who are you trying to fool, Luc?'

'Why should I try to fool you, Verity?' he said softly, his mouth twisting without humour. 'Truly, this is the least I can do in the memory of a very good friend, and his sadly bereaved fiancée, *no es verdad*?'

CHAPTER TWO

WITHOUT waiting for further argument, Luc man-handled Verity's suitcase easily from the back of the jeep and set off towards the hotel entrance, leaving her glaring after his rangy lope, confusion and resentment welling up inside her.

'Luc...*Luc!*' She catapulted herself out of the jeep and ran after him, jet lag forgotten. 'Wait a minute, slow down...'

By the time he turned to inspect her flushed cheeks, he'd already paused at Reception to talk to a girl with curly black hair who was smiling a welcome.

'*Ola*, Señor García!'

Luc's smile flashed white in his dark face. '*Ola*, Maria. Verity, this is Maria. Maria, meet Miss Verity Lacey.'

Slowly, Verity walked the rest of the way across the marble-tiled reception hall, which was full of leafy plants in stone urns. She held out a reluctant hand, and she and Maria greeted each other politely.

'You want the keys to Villa Laguna?' Maria enquired.

Luc nodded. 'And I doubt if Miss Lacey wants to be disturbed until at least midday tomorrow,' he added smoothly.

'On the contrary, I shall be up with the lark!' she said flatly, smiling briefly at Maria before following Luc's rapid progress through an inner courtyard, where a fountain splashed, and then out into a poolside bar and restaurant area. She was too preoccupied to get more than a fleeting impression of tranquil luxury—definitely

25

no cut-price destination, this—with white-coated waiters skimming efficiently between candle-lit tables and clusters of elegant guests.

Several of the waiters nodded deferentially towards Luc as they passed, politely murmuring '*Buenas noches*, Señor García.' Finally catching up with Luc as he wended a determined path through fragrant bushes and palm trees, she realised she'd only done so because he'd stopped outside a white, bougainvillaea-clad villa, perched alone on the edge of a moonlit beach.

Luc's face was in darkness. For a few seconds, she glared at his shadowy expression, indignation vying with her awareness of the peace all around her, the lap and suck of the waves on the white sand, the wind rustling the palm leaves.

'Luc, I'm not at all happy about this!' she began resentfully, as he slid a key into the lock and the arched wooden door swung inwards. As he clicked on the light inside, illuminating a spacious split-level room with pale, rattan furniture, she saw to her increased fury that he was apparently having difficulty suppressing his amusement.

'You may think this is terribly funny,' she began hotly, as he began to laugh in earnest, 'but I find it . . . *humiliating*.'

'Humiliating?' Luc echoed unsympathetically, depositing her case in the middle of the room, and strolling nonchalantly to unfasten the patio doors which opened out on to the beach. 'How so, Verity? In what way do you find my birthday gift to you "humiliating"?'

Eyes flashing, she strode over to stand beside him at the open doorway, ignoring the sensual fan of the trade winds whispering in off the ocean.

'Luc...you and I hardly *know* each other!' she burst out impotently. 'Yet...yet ever since Edward died, you've been playing the part of...of fairy godfather! You've used your influence to help my business...and now you get me out here on the pretext of a working holiday, and I find I'm expected to laze around for almost two weeks instead. Luc, for heaven's sake, what is so *damn* funny?'

'You are.' He stepped out on to a wide, paved terrace, and leaned against the wooden railing. He'd stopped laughing, but his mouth still twitched in amusement. 'Most females of my acquaintance would faint with joy at such despicable treatment!'

She felt hot colour sting her cheeks.

'Knowing the kind of women you *acquaint* yourself with, that doesn't surprise me!' Verity snapped, then felt appalled at herself. Luc's brilliant blue gaze had narrowed in wry interest.

'Yet you say we hardly know each other, Verity,' he mused. 'How can you know what kind of women I acquaint myself with?'

'The circles you move in like to publicise their activities, don't they?'

The mocking gaze was unfathomable suddenly. After a fractional pause, Luc swung away to stare out towards the dark sea. Verity's eyes were drawn involuntarily to the lean, powerful lines of his shoulders and back, the flat hardness of athlete's muscles outlined beneath the clinging white fabric of his T-shirt.

Bearing in mind that she'd privately resolved to forget the past, and since Luc had done nothing but pour help and assistance her way for the last twelve months, she felt bewildered by the angry stir of emotions he was triggering inside her.

But if she'd made up her mind to put their past differences out of her mind, Luc seemed bent on resurrecting everything. What other construction could she put on this crazy situation? And how *dared* he claim he wanted to check she was all right, twelve months on? Like ripping open a recently healed wound to analyse the process of healing...the man was a self-centred sadist! But hadn't she always known that? The facts she'd discovered about him during their brief meeting in Florida last March more than confirmed her opinion...

'Luc, I'm sorry,' she began again, stiffly, striving for calm, 'I'm not meaning to be ungrateful—it's just that...I *know* why you're doing all this, and you don't need to...'

He turned slowly round again, lolling with his elbows behind him on the rail, the muscles rippling on the rock-hard plane of his chest as he did so. With a dry throat, she tore her eyes away from the physical details of Luc García's undeniable sexuality, and concentrated on the cool smile in his eyes, which proved no easier.

'But you hardly know me,' he mimicked softly, the hard mouth twisting again in mockery. 'So how do you know why I'm doing this, Verity?'

'It's obvious. Out of...out of a sense of *guilt*!' she said shakily.

The taut silence which followed threatened to totally wipe out her composure. Even the shrilling of the crickets took on an ominous note. Eventually, with a magnificent shrug, Luc levered himself upright and dug his hands into his pockets, his shuttered gaze impossible to penetrate.

'Guilt? Is that what you really think?'

It wasn't easy deciphering his mood, she decided edgily.

'Yes! Of course it is! What other motive could you possibly have for all this... this patronising benevolence? I mean, until just before my wedding date, we'd never even met, and yet, ever since, you've taken all this... this *paternal* interest in me!'

Luc's expression had grown bleaker.

'Paternal?' he queried laconically. 'You are twenty-two? Twenty-three tomorrow?'

How on earth did he know her exact age? she wondered indignantly. But she nodded stiffly.

'And I am thirty-three. So, unless I was fathering offspring at the tender age of—er—ten, that seems a somewhat unlikely accusation.'

'Oh, stop being pedantic. You know what I mean...' Verity pushed her hands through her hair with a sudden, exhausted gesture, fatigue and jet lag abruptly swamping her. 'You feel you have to pay this... this silly debt of honour in Edward's memory, because you feel guilty about *abusing* your position as Edward's friend and prospective best man! Isn't that it?'

There was another long, charged silence.

'Because of the way I behaved on the terrace of the polo club that night?' Luc murmured, with a wry twist of his lips.

'Yes!'

'And which of us still feels the most guilt, I wonder?'

'That's not fair, Luc!' Verity's cheeks were on fire. Oh, why had she come? Why hadn't she followed her first instincts, and told Luc to go to hell?

'All right.' Luc nodded abruptly, his normally negligible Spanish accent stronger. 'Let us agree on one thing. I have always felt I owed it to Edward to make sure you came to no harm, Verity.'

'*Really*?' For some reason, hearing Luc admit this was like a two-edged sword, scything through Verity's emotions with bewildering results. What else had she expected to hear? she wondered briefly, confused at the unexpected turn her reactions were taking.

'Are you hungry?' Luc's tone was terse. 'Shall I get something sent over from the restaurant?'

Neat change of subject, she reflected angrily. Luc sauntered towards her and reached to take her arm, steering her back inside, and his touch sent a soft shiver across the surface of her skin. Unnerved, she flinched away involuntarily, shaking her head.

'No, I'm not hungry. I'm thirsty and sleepy. If you'll excuse me, I think I'll just grab a fruit juice and collapse into bed.'

'Of course. Let me show you the kitchen. The fridge is well stocked. But I've arranged for maid service. Just pick up the phone and order whatever you like from the hotel.'

She glanced at him as they reached the kitchen, which was airy and light with bleached wooden units.

'You seem to be on very familiar terms with the hotel staff?' she queried flatly, keeping her eyes averted from the disturbing intensity of those dark-lashed blue eyes fixed lazily on her.

'I am,' he agreed tonelessly, 'I employ them.'

'You *employ* them?' she echoed, her jaw dropping. 'You mean this hotel is yours? You own it?'

The wedge of black hair had flopped forward over Luc's forehead, and he lifted a long brown hand to push it slowly back.

'I own it,' he nodded calmly. 'I've also owned a ranch on the island for some time. I breed horses there.'

Verity turned away, not trusting herself to speak. He owned a hotel on this island? And yet he'd had the nerve to suggest he needed a caterer to organise a couple of dinner parties?

'If you don't mind, I'd like to go to bed now.'

The silence behind her made her turn again, to catch a sudden dance of amusement in the blue eyes which fanned her temper.

'Would you, Verity?' he taunted, a wicked flash of mockery in his smile. 'I assume that's a statement, not an invitation?'

Luc's amusement deepened as scarlet colour surged into her face once again.

'Goodnight!' she managed to retort, unsure how she managed to refrain from hitting him.

Danger signals were flashing hectically, making her physically aware of him to an alarming degree. Luc García was the most notorious womaniser she knew. His attitude to the female of the species was cavalier in the extreme. Look at the way he'd behaved last year! But surely he wasn't seriously about to turn his attention on her?

'Don't look so fierce,' Luc advised her calmly, reaching to twist her hot face up for an insultingly casual inspection. 'I will not try to prove anything tonight, Verity. *Hasta mañana. Que duermas bien.*'

When he'd gone, she stood stock-still in the centre of the kitchen, her empty glass in her hand, struggling to identify the welter of emotions whirling around inside her. Anger, indignation at his cool, arrogant self-confidence... plus a vague, indefinable ache inside her which somehow defied analysis. Finally, she gave up. A cool shower and bed. That's what she needed, urgently. She was so tired, she suspected that she could, in fact, sleep the clock round, just as Luc had predicted. But the agitation he'd aroused in her somehow kept sleep at bay, even after the soothing shower followed by a fragrant application of her favourite apple and almond body lotion, and a blissful collapse on to a cool green-and-white-covered bed.

The fan on the ceiling whirred hypnotically as she lay flat on her back, staring at the impossibly black sky outside the window, with its wildly extravagant jewellery of stars. It was too warm for the thin apricot silk night-shirt she'd brought, and she shrugged it off after a while, closing the shutters as a privacy precaution, and lay naked in the darkness.

Tomorrow was her birthday. No, today. It was gone midnight. In fact, if she'd stayed in England, it would have been her birthday for at least five hours, wouldn't it? Sleep-fuddled, she gave up trying to sort that one out. Shifting position, she lifted the unwelcome warmth of her heavy hazel-gold curls from her shoulders, pushing her hair up so that it fanned out in careless disarray over the pillow, then restlessly rolled on to her side and drew one long, silken thigh up to her breasts, linking her arms around her leg. Luc's parting shot tonight was still nig-gling in the back of her mind. He wouldn't try to *prove* anything tonight? A jolt of apprehension surged through her, memories of last year pressing in on her in-exorably... memories of that humiliating night at the polo club ball.

The worst part had been the feel of dancing with Luc, devastating in white dinner-jacket, his lean hardness moving against her through the fine, shimmery gold of her strapless ballgown... He'd been drinking cham-pagne all evening, the ruthless blue gaze gradually ac-quiring a reckless, dangerous glitter as he watched her dancing. He'd known she couldn't stop herself from watching him, just as he'd seemed unable to stop himself from watching her...

She'd been trying and hilariously failing to dance the Lambada with Edward when Luc had cut in. Abruptly the music had changed to a slow, moody ballad, and the warm, cosy, reassuring closeness she'd been experiencing in Edward's arms had switched to that predatory, frightening tension in Luc's... She hadn't thought it possible for such a contrasting set of emotions to tear through her body. Heat had mounted, a silent, growing tension during that physical contact on the dance-floor, until, with a shiver of fear, she'd torn herself away and escaped outside to cool her flushed cheeks, gulp some air into her lungs...

Luc had appeared behind her, a few minutes later. She could still see the dark mask of his face as he twisted her slowly round, raked that probing gaze the length of her body, and then bent to tease her parted lips with his mouth, crushing her soft gasp of protest back inside her mouth with a hungry skill that left her shuddering with mindless desire...

She should have stopped it, right then, but instead her hands, entirely of their own volition, had crept up across the breadth of his shoulders, and into the thick dark silk of his hair, and, with a husky growl of triumph, Luc's hands had moulded the narrow expanse of her ribcage, cupping her breasts with consummate skill and then sliding down to caress her back, moulding the taut jut of her buttocks, gluing their bodies together with a rough urgency which left neither in any doubt of their unspoken desire for each other...

Voices at the other end of the terrace had finally brought her back to her senses, with a jolt of appalled self-disgust. With a choked gasp she'd broken away from him, turned to make a blind, headlong flight for the sanctuary of the ladies' room . . .

Verity gave a groan of anguish in the dark silence of the bedroom, and rolled convulsively on to her stomach, fresh guilt flowing through her. Edward had known nothing of what had happened that evening. He'd been at the bar, drinking and telling jokes with a crowd of fellow polo players. But how *could* she have experienced that feeling in Luc's arms, when she was wearing Edward's engagement ring? Admittedly, she'd shunned Luc like the plague for the remainder of that week. She'd been so determined to be faithful to Edward, to compensate for her momentary lapse of common sense, she'd found the flimsiest of excuses to avoid further contact with his 'friend' Luc. She'd pleaded commitments to the family she worked for, even feigned a sudden attack of migraine. She'd succeeded in evading any further confrontation with Luc García until the minimal, icily formal dealings following the nightmare of Edward's death . . .

But, even so, morally, mentally, she'd been unfaithful, hadn't she? Even if it was only for a few seconds? And what had made the anguish a hundred times worse was Edward's sudden accident, Edward's death . . . She'd never had the chance to prove to herself and to the arrogant Luc García that she *did* love her fiancé, that she'd every intention of marrying him, of enjoying a secure happy life as Edward's wife . . .

Why had Luc suddenly decided to fly her out here to fulfil some misguided obligation? To insist that she relaxed? Relaxing was the last thing she wanted to do. Relaxing gave her too much time to think. If she kept busy, she could blot out the memories, she could keep them at bay . . .

*   *   *

She wasn't sure exactly when she fell asleep, but she woke to a sun-filled room, and experienced a few seconds of total disorientation before remembering where she was. Of course, she was hundreds of miles from the grey northern skies of London. She was in the Dominican Republic. In a villa in the grounds of Luc García's hotel, with stripes of golden sunshine filtering through the slatted shutters on the window...

Stretching tentatively, and yawning, she decided that she felt remarkably refreshed. The disturbing emotions connected with Edward's memory had faded to bearable proportions in the bright light of morning. It wasn't in Verity's nature to brood or look on the pessimistic side. She had a calm, resilient side to her nature which had survived intact despite some hefty knocks in the last few years...

In the back of her mind she still felt furious at Luc's overbearing patronage. But a good night's sleep always had a miraculous power to restore her spirits. And there was a quality of peaceful anticipation about her surroundings that seemed to expel last night's dark thoughts, making it impossible to feel angry or resentful, making her want to jump out of bed and explore her new surroundings without a care in the world.

It was a pity she'd have to go home tomorrow. But at least she could enjoy today, and to hell with Luc García and his hard, mocking blue eyes...

A luxurious bathroom led off the bedroom, with a pale green suite which blended elegantly with the bedroom decorations. Fluffy green towels and natural wood cupboards completed the effect. Verity rapidly showered, fastened her hazel curls on top of her head and, having riffled through her suitcase to don a yellow and white flower-patterned bikini and matching T-shirt dress, flung open the shutters and gave a gasp of stunned delight at the scene which met her eyes.

Arriving last night in the dark, she'd had only the vaguest impression of a tropical paradise. This morning, framed in the window like a glossy poster, lay a crescent of white beach, an endless expanse of blue-green sea, and acres of lush green palm trees shimmering their fronds in the breeze.

Filled with impatience to run across that sugar-white sand to the sea, she snatched her sunglasses and pattered barefoot through the villa to the patio-doors which led to the terrace, then halted in her tracks, her stomach tightening involuntarily.

Luc García lazed in a rattan chair, clad only in white Bermuda shorts, eyes slitted against the sun as he gazed out across the bay. Beside him was a white-clothed rattan table, set for breakfast with silver cutlery and condiments, baskets of rolls and fruit, and a cut-glass vase of delicately waxen flowers as a centre-piece, like creamy narcissi with smudgy yellow centres.

'Good morning,' he purred, barely moving a muscle. 'Happy birthday, Verity.'

'Good morning, Luc.' She forced herself forward with an unconcerned smile, but her heart was thudding as if she'd just jogged along the beach. She felt sick with nervous apprehension. Was this an elaborate seduction plan? Had Luc García suddenly decided to expand on what had, up till now, been a casual acquaintance and one illicit, champagne-induced aberration? His gibe last night about proving something…was *that* what this was all about? Proving that he only had to snap his fingers and she was his for the taking? Verity felt her bubbly joy of a few seconds ago beginning to fade. There was no way, no chance at all, that she could risk any kind of involvement with him...especially not the kind of no-strings, shallow variety of relationship he seemed to specialise in.

The brilliant gaze was strangely shuttered as she joined him at the table. She felt glad of the protective anonymity of her sunglasses as she pulled out a chair and sat down cautiously, as far away from him as possible.

'Still on your high horse, Verity?' he taunted, with a hard twist of his mouth.

She gave a cool shrug, reaching out for a mango, and slicing it open.

'Of course not.'

The juicy yellow flesh glistened invitingly in the sun, and she picked up a spoon and began to dig out the fruit and eat it slowly, too tense to fully enjoy the exotic flavour.

'What else would you like?' Luc was watching her with lidded eyes, his presence making it impossible for her to concentrate on her own thoughts. There was a hint of danger emanating from his motionless pose by the table.

The naked breadth of his chest, tanned and hair-roughened, the ridges of muscle flat yet supple, made her feel flustered. In spite of her denial, she did feel angry with him—quite illogically so—simply for having this effect on her.

'Rolls and fruit are fine,' she said quickly.

'Coffee? Hot croissants?'

'All right, yes...thank you.'

Luc stood up, briefly mesmerising her with the play of rock-like muscle beneath the silken brown of thighs and shoulders, and strolled into the villa to phone the order through to the hotel. Taking a deep, steadying breath, Verity raked a trembling hand into her hair and rested her elbow on the table, staring blankly at the exquisite flowers in the vase.

'What are these?' she asked Luc, as he came back.

'Frangipani. Do you like them?'

She nodded quickly. 'They're beautiful... Luc, how long have you been sitting outside the villa?'

A fleeting quirk of humour touched his mouth, but not, she felt certain, his eyes.

'Not too long. I went snorkelling over on the coral reef, and when I came out of the water I was hungry. I had the table laid out here in case you woke up and joined me for breakfast.'

'What if I hadn't?'

He shrugged. 'Then I would have had the table re-laid for lunch.'

Verity rubbed her nose, frowning slightly. 'But *why*?' she burst out, unable to help herself. Immediately she'd asked, she felt herself reddening. If Luc had previously suspected her of being naïve, now he'd have good reason, she decided nervously. What other construction could she possibly put on all this? It *had* to be his famed seduction routine.

'To wish you a happy birthday, Verity. A happier birthday than last year...'

'You could just have sent me a birthday card,' she pointed out with as much calm as she could muster, flipping off her sunglasses and fixing a candid gaze on him. 'If you'd wanted to be really generous you could even have sent me a bunch of flowers, or a box of chocolates!'

The blue gaze was unflinching on the wide, questioning gold-brown of Verity's. There was a lengthy pause before Luc finally switched subjects with abrupt lack of warning.

'Does it upset you to talk about Edward?'

Caught off-guard, she laid down her spoon with a hand that trembled slightly.

'No... Of course not. I've never wanted to pretend he never existed. The... the advice I got was talk about it as much as I could... I'd come to terms with it better that way...'

Luc was watching her silently, and Verity felt her stomach clench at the flicker of cynicism in his eyes. Or was she imagining it? Was her own guilty conscience making her look for meanings that didn't exist?

'Edward was a good friend of mine,' he said finally. 'He helped me through a bad time in my life. I never forgot his support.'

Verity waited, resentment warring with curiosity, debating whether to probe, then deciding it wiser not to. The darkening of Luc's eyes warned at some painful event in his past which he wouldn't readily expose to casual curiosity. But all she could think of was the arrogant way Luc had treated her, when she'd been Edward's fiancée, when Edward had trusted him enough to invite him to be best man at his wedding. Had that been Luc's idea of repaying Edward for this mysterious help and support in the past?

'He was very much in love with you,' he went on grimly, 'but you already know that. Don't you?'

She nodded stiffly. Colour warmed her cheeks. What was he driving at? Did he know how it had been between her and Edward? Had he seen straight through her cowardly motives for choosing happiness and security over the kind of deep, all-consuming passion which terrified her?

'What is the point you are trying to make?' she demanded unevenly, avoiding those penetrating eyes.

'He told me how your parents were killed together in a climbing accident. So, when he died too——'

'You thought your "best man" duties should still apply?' she cut in, with a tight smile. 'You felt obliged to keep a distant eye on the poor little orphan and bereaved fiancée thereafter? Tell me, did you have this personal little chat about me before or after you tried to *seduce* me on the terrace that night?'

Luc studied her angry smile, and his answering smile held a darker gleam.

'*Seduce* you, Verity? Aren't you forgetting that English expression, "It takes two to tango?"' The gleam became more ruthlessly mocking.

'You haven't answered my question!'

'Does it make any difference? Are you keen to know if I really found you irresistible? Or whether I was testing you, to check out your true feelings for Edward?'

Verity felt a surge of blind anger at Luc's scarcely concealed contempt. So *that* was it! Luc's opinion of women was so low that he'd imagined it necessary to *test* Edward's fiancée for future fidelity! It made a sick kind of sense, now she thought about it. It was the cold-blooded, premeditated style of behaviour typical of Luc García's appalling track record... When she thought of what she'd discovered about him, during her time in Florida last year, about his actions in the past, his treatment of his wife, the hardest thing of all to believe was that Edward could ever have befriended such a man.

She opened her mouth to spit out her true feelings, then swallowed hard before she could say things she knew she would regret. Who was she to stand in judgement on Luc? She *had* felt a wave of purely physical attraction towards him. She couldn't deny that agonising episode between them last year. She'd never forgive herself for it, even though she would never have allowed it to develop, even though she knew very well that her relationship with Edward was all that she wanted, all that she could ever commit herself to...

There was an implacable light in Luc's eyes as he watched her wrestling with her bruised emotions, and, casting wildly around for a life-saving reason to control her temper, she recalled the business he'd passed to her over the last twelve months, and Sara's words of caution before she left. If the assistance over the past year had been his version of an olive-branch, she was guilty of accepting it, profiting from it... She at least owed him a degree of civility.

She expelled her breath sharply, shaking her head.

'No! You're quite right, it makes no difference! It's all over and done with. I'd rather draw a discreet veil over the whole thing, if you don't mind.'

'But I seem to have upset you again,' Luc murmured wryly, not sounding in the least apologetic. 'This wasn't at all what I had in mind for your birthday celebrations.'

'What *did* you have in mind, Luc?'

He appeared oblivious to her cutting tone.

'This morning—snorkelling. The water is perfect...'

'I haven't a clue how to snorkel.'

'*No hay problema*. I'll teach you. This afternoon—the choice is yours.'

'Big of you!'

He ignored her. 'We could go back into Puerto Plata, take the cable car up Isabel de Torres mountain. There's a wonderful view from up there. Or I could show you the mangroves in Gri Gri Lagoon on the way to Rio San Juan, cattle country.' He paused, glancing at her set face with a shrug. 'Or perhaps that could wait until tomorrow.

My ranch is near there. And the field where I play polo when I am on the island...'

'Hold on!' Verity couldn't take any more of this high-handed planning of her time. 'Forget tomorrow! I'll have a quick look at the island today, but tomorrow I fly home!'

Luc held her angry gaze steadily, his own lidded and laughing.

'*Creo que no,*' he taunted softly. 'I think not. Calm yourself, Verity. We owe it to Edward to be friends, to forget the past...'

'Just how do you arrive at that...*convoluted* conclusion?' she demanded shakily, abruptly jumping to her feet, her resolve to control her temper totally forgotten. 'I've no intention of forgetting the past. The past taught me valuable lessons! I still feel badly about what happened that night last March.'

'You have a guilty conscience?' Luc purred, eyes narrowed on her flushed cheeks. She wanted to kick him, he looked so still and controlled in the face of her agitation.

'You haven't *got* a conscience!' she flung back in a low, furious voice, stung by the subtle inflexion in his voice. 'And I realise all this unwarranted attention you're turning on me is some kind of twisted debt of honour, a sense of obligation, because you were Edward's friend. Some friend! He'd have been better off without your so-called friendship, and so would I!'

'Do you feel guilty because you didn't fight me off as thoroughly as you thought you should,' Luc persisted, his voice hardening, 'or because, for a few seconds, you found yourself wanting to make love with me, when you were engaged to marry Edward?'

'That's not true!'

'No?' Luc slowly stood up, and Verity found him standing so close to her that she couldn't breathe; he stood, looming, tall and dark, the coarse strength of his naked chest far too close for peace of mind.

When she did catch her breath, it was the scent of Luc's skin, warm from the sun, which seemed to fill her nostrils. He smelled of sea-salt, and spice and honey. Shivers of reaction were spreading all over her body. She tried to take a step back, but her chair was in the way. When Luc reached to take her hand, pulling her determinedly against him, she wrapped the other arm across her breasts in unconscious defence. She could feel an overwhelming ache of desire melting her anger, tightening her nipples beneath the soft fabric of her bikini, and T-shirt. Mortified, she clawed back her composure with desperation.

'No, it's not true! Just because you have the kind of looks which send hordes of females into ecstasies, you think you're invincible! You imagine every woman you meet is going to fall at your feet...'

'You really think so?' Luc murmured with a slight quirk of his mouth, his narrowed blue gaze intent on the fullness of her parted lips. 'It's an entertaining fantasy.'

'You took me by surprise, that night! That was all!' she said jerkily, taut as a reed in his arms. 'I felt nothing for you then, and I feel nothing for you now!'

'So if I kissed you now, you'd feel nothing?' The light in Luc's eyes had intensified. She imagined the gleam in a lion's eyes before pouncing on its prey.

'Correct! Just as you'd feel nothing!' she shot back in a choked voice.

'So, just to lay old ghosts, we should put this theory to the test, shouldn't we?' A husky note had deepened his voice to a sensual growl.

'No! Luc, I don't think that's necessary...'

'No?'

He'd closed the already narrowed space between them and was easing her tauntingly against him. But instead of bending his head to seek her mouth with his he merely gazed at her parted lips, his eyes darkening beneath narrowed lids as the pupils dilated with banked-down desire. The suspended action was silent agony. Verity felt as if every nerve-end in her body was raw. Every pulse was racing hectically. But she stayed frozen, motionless in his arms, a steel clamp on her emotions, almost dizzy with the swamp of physical awareness she was suppressing.

When he finally lowered his mouth to cover hers, the sensation was devastating. His lips moved on hers in a light, skilful caress, tasting and seeking, sending tremors of reaction shuddering through her from head to toe. Holding back her instinctive desire to crush herself against him felt like the fiercest battle she'd ever fought.

'Satisfied?' she hissed unsteadily, as he loosened his hold on her slightly, his fingers still circling her arms.

'More than satisfied,' Luc drawled softly, his gaze as ambiguous as his words. His eyes travelled down over the tender swell of her breasts, beneath her T-shirt, down over the curve of her hips and the slender length of her thighs, right down to her narrow ankles and high insteps. The peach-painted tips of her toes tensed under that burning scrutiny.

She opened her mouth to challenge him, but just then a white-jacketed waiter appeared through the lush screen of palms surrounding the villa, bearing a tray with a tall silver coffee service and aromatic croissants.

Luc released her, and she stepped back from him so quickly that she almost bumped into the table.

'*Buenos días, señor, señorita...*' The young man flashed them a glistening white smile.

Deeply relieved at the interruption, Verity smiled back at him rather more enthusiastically than she would normally have done, and the man looked gratified.

'*Gracias*, Pablito,' Luc said abruptly. Verity noted his displeasure with a stab of unholy triumph.

When the waiter had gone, she sat down again at the table, and began calmly to pour some coffee, cursing her trembling hand. Could Luc see how much she was shaking?

'How do you like your coffee?' she enquired politely.

'Black, no sugar.'

She passed him the cup, and poured herself a white one. Luc had sat down again too. He was watching her through half-closed eyes, his expression impossible to read.

'Since we have just proved our mutual indifference so... conclusively,' he said at last, his deep voice sardonic, 'let's also dispense with the hysterics and the guilt complexes. There is no need for this show of proud outrage and resentment. You will not fly home tomorrow, because to do so would not only waste a holiday opportunity, but it would deprive me of your creative skills for an important entertaining function...'

'I'll fly home when I damn well choose! With you being in the hotel trade, you must have dozens of experienced caterers at your disposal! This is a farcical situation!'

Luc drained his coffee-cup and stood up, eyeing her glittering gaze and flushed cheeks with an infuriating lack of emotion.

'Now that you are here,' he assured her with supreme arrogance, 'you will stay. The island will bewitch you.' He gestured lazily towards the white sand and the endless stretch of blue water, before turning to leave. 'Finish your breakfast and meet me on the beach in half an hour. I'll show you the coral reef. By the end of the week, you'll be hooked for life!'

Seething with resentment, Verity could only glare after him as he sauntered away and disappeared through the palm trees, as nonchalant and confident as if they'd just parted best of friends.

CHAPTER THREE

'I DON'T know why I'm letting you bully me into this,' Verity protested, the sun hot on her back as she waded back to the shallows beside Luc after her first attempt at snorkelling. 'If I'm going to spend any time at all here, I'd be better off scouring the local markets, finding local recipes. At least then I'd take something useful back with me...'

'Forget business,' Luc told her mockingly, his eyes roaming over the pale tautness of her body in the yellow and white floral swimsuit. When he reached to flick the strap of her bikini-top aside, she gasped and flinched away.

'Just checking for sunburn,' Luc explained blandly, tilting an enquiring eyebrow at her nervous reaction. 'You can burn underwater. Did you use a waterproof sun-lotion?'

'Yes! I'm not totally witless...'

'Possibly not. In fact, I'd say you were quite intelligent,' he taunted with a merciless grin. 'But your problem is an inability to relax. That's why you're here, remember?'

'So you keep telling me!'

'And so you keep forgetting.'

'This afternoon I'll hire a car, explore the whole island, get as many original recipes as I can to take home with me——'

'Slow down, Verity! This is the land of *mañana*. Here people take their time, move at an easy pace. And ex-

47

ploring the entire Dominican Republic is a little am-
bitious. It's the second largest West Indian state. Nearly
forty-nine thousand square kilometres of it.'

They'd reached the soft white sand, and Luc stopped
and caught her arm, sitting down and pulling her down
beside him. She fought off that shivering, sinking feeling
in her stomach, and surreptitiously widened the space
between them. The fine sand stuck to her thighs, but it
was so hot that her swimsuit was almost dry.

Luc's long, muscled body was uncomfortably close,
the flesh lean and darkly tanned and hair-roughened.
He was dangerously masculine, dangerously disturbing
in his brief navy-blue swimming-trunks. Woodenly she
stared out at the shimmering ocean, suppressing her
wayward thoughts, even suppressing the wayward bubble
of pleasure as she recalled the secret underwater world
she'd just visited for the first time. She'd no wish to
enthuse girlishly about it to Luc. Tolerating his company
was the only concession she intended.

'I didn't mean examine every corner of the island! I'd
settle for a quick tour round this immediate area. I'll
have to see about hiring a car.'

'There's no need to hire a car. I'm at your disposal,
señorita. Guide and chauffeur.'

'Thanks. But I'd rather go alone. There's no need for
you to bother.'

'It's no bother. I know the island well. It feels a second
home to me. My ancestors date back to the early Spanish
colonialists.'

His drawl was undeterred, and subtly mocking.

'So shall we go west, back into Puerto Plata? Or east,
out to my ranch, and the polo field?'

'Puerto Plata will be fine.' It was the only thing she
could say. If she kept up the argument, she'd be under-

mining her claim of indifference towards him. And she had no wish to see Luc playing polo. She hadn't been to a polo match since Edward died ...

'Puerto Plata it is, then. And tonight we'll have dinner here at the hotel.'

Verity frowned slightly, her heart sinking at the prospect of a whole day in Luc's disturbing company.

'Luc—don't you have other things to do?'

'No.' His smile was bland, with a hint of mockery again. 'I am entirely at your disposal, Señorita Lacey.'

There was a direct, narrowed challenge in the lazy gaze directed at her. What he really meant was, she was entirely at his mercy! Glaring at him in wary resignation, Verity turned away, afraid of what he might read in her eyes.

'Lucky me!' she murmured, attempting to hide her agitation with dry sarcasm.

But, despite her reluctance to let Luc take control in this high-handed way, as the day unfolded in a lazy pattern of swimming and sunbathing and exploring, Verity found herself beginning to grudgingly review her luck. The water was warm, and, with a further short course of patient instruction from Luc, snorkelling proved a delight. The slow, easy atmosphere of the island seeped into her senses. It was impossible, she decided, to stay stiff and tense in the humid heat of a tropical island. Luc, taken at face value, was addictive company. Relaxed, knowledgeable, witty, an excellent guide and a skilful instructor.

They had lunch in Puerto Plata, where Luc introduced her to *katifrittos*, deep-fried pastries with a filling of spicy minced meat. She politely declined the alarming-sounding choices of deep-fried chicken's feet, or stuffed intestines. But the *katifrittos* were delicious, and she told Luc so, adding that she must get the recipe.

They were eating on the terrace of a harbour-front restaurant, beneath the shady canopy of bamboo pergola and palm trees. The Atlantic ocean glittered sliver-blue on one side, the mountain Luc had proposed they visit towering high above them on the other.

'Business talk is forbidden,' he reminded her solemnly.

She crossed one slender leg over the other, absently smoothing her fingers over the cotton drill of her yellow Bermudas, and sipped her drink thoughtfully.

'If you think for one moment that I'm going to pass up the chance of collecting new ideas for Verity Lacey Catering, you're mistaken!' she shot back, unrepentant. 'I might try to get a licence to import this amazing green coconut milk, for example!' She waved her glass at him determinedly. 'My business is my life. Just the way polo is yours!'

Luc raised a dark eyebrow. 'Polo hardly constitutes my entire life, Verity.'

'No?' She shrugged. 'Well, apart from the Hotel Laguna, it must do. You travel all year, playing in different parts of the world. You have a ranch here, but that's where presumably you breed polo ponies? Oh, I suppose you mean you have other *hobbies*—your coterie of female admirers!'

'What a shallow and pointless existence you've decreed for me,' he murmured wryly. 'Do you want dessert?' He was signalling to the waiter.

'Just fruit, I think. And coffee. I'm paying, by the way.'

Luc's answering glance contained such steely stubbornness that she felt her heart sinking.

'You are my guest,' he said shortly.

'Yes, but if I'm not allowed to work my way I'm damn well going to pay it!'

'What do you suggest?' he queried tauntingly, his eyes darkening to an ominous shade. Against the dark blue of the polo shirt he'd slung on that morning over his white shorts, the narrowed irises appeared a rich dark navy. 'A part-time job in my hotel? Commis-chef? Chambermaid?'

'I'm not sure I'm staying! But if I do I wouldn't mind working as an assistant chef in your hotel kitchen, or taking on any other job you care to mention!' she shot back acidly.

'Indeed?' He leaned back, tapping a long brown finger on the white table-top. 'Perhaps I should capitalise on such a generous offer?' The gleam in his eyes warned her he was mocking. 'Maybe I could put you on stand-by as my temporary... personal assistant?'

Verity could feel her face growing hotter. The look in Luc's eyes was suddenly deeply disturbing.

'I'd need a more detailed job description,' she countered flatly.

'Relax, remember?' he drawled, after a lengthy pause had stretched out between them. 'You're too tense, Verity. Too serious. Where's your sense of humour?'

'Back in London,' Verity admitted, dropping her eyes from his penetrating gaze and switching to the glorious view beyond the terrace.

Luc's voice held a different note when he asked abruptly, 'Is there some man back in London you're involved with? Have I unwittingly torn you from a new love-affair?'

It was impossible to decipher his tone. He sounded casual, almost dismissive. Verity felt she could stand no more of this interference. Luc might have the best of altruistic intentions, or he might be playing cat and mouse with her. Either way, her private life was none of his business.

'Let's just say I don't feel we're close enough acquaintances to merit an intimate discussion on my personal life!' she told him calmly. 'Whisking me out here at your expense doesn't give you the right to pry...'

She was within her rights to say it, but somehow she felt a wave of remorse. With a slight shake of her head, she smiled uncertainly at Luc.

'But I'm sorry—I am enjoying today. I didn't mean to sound...bitchy. Can we talk about something else?'

'Of course. Let's call another truce, shall we?' Luc's face was sardonic. 'Did you enjoy the snorkelling out on the reef?'

'It was wonderful!' Verity admitted, feeling a reluctant glow engulf her as she recalled it. 'I never realised all that beauty was there—isn't that an admission? I loved those yellow and violet branchy things—what did you say they were called?'

'Venus fans.'

'Venus fans...' she repeated gravely, visualising the host of other creatures he'd named. There'd been sea-urchins, and sea-cucumbers, and something called a feather-star—'living fossils' he'd called them—creatures which hadn't changed for millions of years. Then all the brilliantly coloured fish, from tiny minnows to the pairs of angel-fishes, swarms of surgeon-fishes, stick-like trumpet-fishes hunting, and alarmingly big barracudas.

Luc seemed to know a lot about the undersea world. Her gibe about being blinkered by polo struck her suddenly as being rather uncalled for. She bit her lip, but refrained from resurrecting the subject. Best to steer a superficial course through their conversations, she decided. Whenever they veered on to the personal, hostilities broke out again.

'The next thing to learn is scuba-diving,' Luc murmured with a wry smile, watching the enthusiasm lighting up her face. 'You can see much more. When you have spent hours in another world, weightless as a fish, watching the sunlight shifting silently across the ocean floor, forgetting all the problems of the real world, you might even become addicted, like me. But now let's take the cable car up the mountain.'

Luc had settled the bill before she had time to make a stand, and when he came around the table and put a hand lightly on her bare shoulder to steer her out of the restaurant she jerked as if he'd administered an electric shock.

Twisting away from his touch, she avoided his searching scrutiny. At the end of the street, Luc stopped her, catching hold of her arm again and pulling her round to face him.

'Verity...we agreed that there is nothing, not a spark of attraction, between us,' he taunted implacably. 'And yet you shy away like a nervous horse each time I touch you. Am I repulsive to you?'

'*Repulsive*?' she echoed involuntarily, then stopped, aware that she was under intent, mocking scrutiny. Her face grew hot suddenly, and she caught her breath at the flicker of cynical knowledge in Luc's eyes, wishing he'd let go of her arm.

'"Repulsive" might be a little melodramatic,' she managed to retort lightly. 'But I'd prefer it if you kept your hands to yourself!'

Luc slowly released her, lifting his hands in a gesture of mock surrender. 'I will do my very best to remember

that, Verity,' he grated, scanning her flushed face with
unmistakable derision in his hard blue gaze.

Could there be some physical cause of this powerful
emotional reaction she felt for him? she wondered wildly,
as they duly took the cable car up the mountain and
admired the breathtaking view of misty green hills and
endless turquoise seas. Some sort of manifestation of
the law of magnetic attraction and rejection? If she ever
admitted the devastating effect Luc had on her, she'd be
endlessly humiliated...

By the time they got back to the hotel later in the
afternoon, and Luc went off to attend to some hotel
business, her own company was both an immense relief
and a shattering anticlimax. The battle-station emotions
Luc's company triggered off must have left her with an
adrenalin addiction, she decided bleakly. They said war
veterans suffered from it.

Cross with her tense edginess, now that she had time
alone at last, she embarked on a positive plan of relaxation. First a quick swim, then a leisurely bask in the
sun, followed by a doze on her bed until it was time to
shower and change for dinner. The first part was easily
completed, the second was complicated by falling asleep
on a sun-lounger beneath a palm tree on the beach, and
only waking when Pablito tapped her gently on the
shoulder and pointed out that the early Caribbean sunset
was upon them, and it would soon be pitch-dark.

The night seemed full of the mysterious squeaks and
cheepings of nocturnal animals and insects as she walked
back towards the villa, the air heady with perfume.
Making a quick dash for the shower, she emerged tingling
and refreshed, with an inexplicable sense of well-being
despite the rigours of the day in Luc's unnerving
presence, and the forthcoming ordeal of dinner. Maybe

it was the subtle atmosphere of the Caribbean, eroding her defences? One thing was certain, she reflected, as she debated what to wear; she had to relax and ignore Luc's taunts. She had to shrug it all off. If she could survive without a permanent rift, at least she'd have been loyal to Sara and her worries about their catering business...

Confidence dressing, that was what she needed to-night. Something which made a statement, a gesture of defiance in the face of Luc's cool derision. The floral chiffon with the tiny gold straps, she decided finally, extracting it from the case and shaking out any creases. It was slightly *risqué*, the skimpy straps ruling out a bra, but then Luc's opinion of her as a kind of *femme fatale* was already fairly damning, and it was her birthday, after all. That was a perfectly good reason to dress up, quite independent of Luc García...

It was so warm that she settled for leaving her freshly shampooed curls to dry naturally, and, finally slipping her bare feet into the gold high-heeled sandals, she walked thoughtfully to the mirror on the bedroom wall and gazed critically at her reflection.

Her slender figure gazed back, and she frowned slightly, aware that she looked different, almost a stranger to herself. Was it the fairy-tale atmosphere of this place, the far-away-from-it-all feel, that gave her an almost ethereal air, yet at the same time gave her hair a brighter shine, the curves of her figure more emphasis? Or was it much more likely just an increased body awareness, triggered by a day's lazing half-naked in sea and sun, and experiencing new activities?

She smoothed a light film of translucent tawny blusher on her cheeks, and touched her lips with a browny coral lip-pencil. A slick of gold eyeshadow, and a brush of

brown mascara completed her make-up. Finally, slipping
a fine, woven silk gold shawl around her shoulders, she
made her way slowly through the cicada-filled gardens
to the hotel, her emotions regrouping into their battle
formations.

Luc, in light beige dinner-jacket and navy bow-tie, was
sprawled on a bar stool, a drink in one hand, a telephone receiver cradled between shoulder and neck, con-
ducting a low-voiced conversation as she approached.
Catching sight of her, he curtly terminated the conversation in rapid Spanish, handing the phone back to
Pablito behind the bar. The phone rang again, and after
a brief word Pablito held out the receiver to Luc, who
took it absently and then seemed to suspend movement
for a few seconds, the brilliant gaze narrowing as he took
in her appearance.

Walking towards him with all the poise she possessed,
Verity nevertheless felt abruptly self-conscious at the
intent scrutiny she received. The gossamer-fine evening
dress suddenly felt like a transparent nightdress. As the
disturbing blue gaze moved appreciatively down the
length of her body, it took all her powers of self-control
to refrain from glancing down to check that she was
properly dressed for dinner on a hotel terrace.

'*Ola, buenas noches*, Verity,' he murmured, the husky
timbre of his voice more pronounced along with that
elusive 'foreignness' which seemed to wax and wane with
his mood. Was it a deliberate, premeditated ploy of his
when he was trying to decimate female opposition to his
Latin charm? Furious at her shiver of weakness, she
produced one of her most nonchalant smiles in self-
defence.

'Good evening, Luc,' she countered lightly, perching
on the nearest bar stool. 'Don't let me interrupt you . . .'

She turned a dazzling smile on Pablito, who grinned back at her widely, stopping in the act of polishing a glass with a large white napkin as if momentarily arrested by the warm golden glow she projected.

'*Buenas noches, señorita. Qué quiere?*'

'*Ola*, Pablito. May I try one of those, please...?' She flicked a finger at Luc's drink.

Luc, in what sounded like softly annoyed Spanish, spoke on the phone for a few more seconds and then replaced the receiver with an air of controlled finality.

'For the rest of the evening, I am unavailable, Pablito,' he said flatly, turning his attention on Verity, who was blithely sipping her drink. 'How are you enjoying that?'

'Mmm... delicious! What is it?'

'That's a Ron Sour. Rum, lime, egg whites, nutmeg and ice.'

'Well, it's wonderful!' She took another sip, and ran her tongue happily over her lips, sweeping her eyes over the scene on the terrace bar, where elegant guests were beginning to fill the candle-lit tables, and waiters weaved around with menus.

Luc stared at her for a long moment, his eyes enigmatic. Finally, he said coolly, 'You look wonderful.'

'Why, thank you!' She inclined her head to hide the sweep of heat in her cheeks. She was putting on a brilliant performance, she decided, just the right note of blithe indifference.

Luc slid a hand into the inside pocket of his jacket, and withdrew a long, slim package, wrapped in gold paper. He handed it to her, his expression deadpan.

'I was going to wait until we'd had our meal. But now I find I cannot wait. Happy birthday, Verity.' There was something in his eyes, just briefly, which made her catch her breath in her throat. A raw, hungry look which hollowed her stomach, and brought a flood of heat all over her body. The next moment, she decided she'd imagined it. His gaze was shuttered again.

Leaning forward, he kissed her cheek, his lips firm and cool as they brushed her skin in the most discreet embrace, yet still managing to send her pulse-rate haywire.

With nerveless fingers, she took the package and stared at it uncertainly.

'Luc, this is ... I mean, you don't need to buy me a present ...'

'Just open it.'

'OK. But I can't accept it.'

'Yes, you can.' Luc's voice was coolly authoritative.

With a stiff shrug, she took a deep breath and un-wrapped it. Inside a long black leather box was a fine gold pendant, fashioned from an oval-cut jewel which glowed a rich, deep sunset shade, surrounded by smaller glittery-white stones which sparked deep fire in the lights from the bar.

Lifting her eyes, she met Luc's lidded gaze, her throat dry. Presents from Luc? Jewellery, which looked so exquisitely made that it must have cost a fortune? Was this the second phase of the plan? The advance payment for the expected services rendered? His low opinion of her might have given him completely false expectations— did he assume her gratitude would break down any barriers?

Her heart hammering, she decided to play the game his way, for the time being. Fixing a false smile on her face, she stood up and dropped a light kiss on his hard cheek, trembling inside as he reached out and caught her wrist, preventing the quick retreat she'd planned.

'It's lovely, but I can't accept it, Luc!' she said lightly, trying to ease her hand free.

'It is yours. You can wear it now. It goes with the peach and gold material of your dress.' His deep voice was insistent. She swallowed convulsively, reactions tingling up her arm at the firm pressure of his fingers.

'Luc, I can't...'

'But we are old acquaintances,' he reminded her patiently, his tone amused. 'Acquaintances can give each other presents. You can buy me something for my birthday in August. Then we will be even, *es verdad*?'

Slowly he twisted her round, and, taking the pendant from its case, he slid it round her neck, fastening it easily at the nape, his fingers smoothing aside her still damp curls with a light, sure confidence which somehow conjured images of the countless other women he must have performed a similar operation for.

She caught her breath in a combination of anger and resignation, and then looked down at the jewel, which lay softly glowing against her skin, just above the hollow between her breasts, finally lifting the heavy stone to the light, turning it over with a curiosity which overcame her annoyance.

'Since you've gone to the trouble of buying it for me, and you've forcibly fastened it on me, I'll wear it tonight,' she compromised with a shaky laugh, watching the play of light on the jewel. 'It's beautiful, Luc. What *is* it?'

'The yellow stone is amber. This coast is called the Costa d'Ambra. Amber is mined in these mountains.'

'Amber...' She gazed into its glowing depths. 'Luc, I love it. I think it's the most beautiful pendant I've ever seen, but I really can't accept...'

'You have already accepted. *Bueno*! We will go and eat.'

'*Si, patrón*!' she agreed with dry obedience, allowing herself to be escorted to a table in a leafy bower, close to the pool and the floodlit royal palms silhouetted against the night sky.

A group of musicians—four men and two women— had appeared at the far side of the small dance-floor, and with guitar and saxophone they were playing softly rhythmical music which Verity hazarded would become more assertive as the evening progressed. They made an eyecatching sight, the men in shiny gold waistcoats and gold headbands, the women in frilly orange bikini-tops, curvy bare midriffs, and drapy, layered skirts, in vivid, brilliant colours.

Conversation flowed so easily with Luc that Verity wondered if their apparent rapport tonight was the effects of the Ron Sour, or whether she was succumbing to his fatal charm without even realising it.

They talked about London, about her business, about the friends in Luc's circle who now habitually used Verity Lacey Catering for their social functions, almost to the exclusion of any other firm.

No longer sure, after a couple of glasses of wine, whether she was play-acting or not, she found herself describing to him the intense pleasure she derived from the creation of fantasy settings for her clients' parties. Over a delectable meal of crab meat on palm hearts, and crayfish in butter, and then sirloin steak, served with proud panache by the chef, the atmosphere between them grew a little warmer. They exchanged views on books, discovering a shared liking for authors as diverse as Umberto Eco and Agatha Christie, and films and theatre, Luc revealing a liking for two extremes: action-packed adventure-comedy, or the obscure high-brow foreign stuff with sub-titles.

'The Spanish ones are my favourite,' he added, with a wry twist of a smile over his glass of Burgundy. 'But maybe because I have the advantage of being bilingual?'

'That must be it, because I promise you I get annoyed having to read the translations—I miss half the action! Give me a lovely romantic epic any day. The sort where you need a box of tissues in your lap!'

'You, a romantic?' Luc queried, his gaze quizzical across the candle-lit table. Verity caught herself up with a jolt. The cynicism was back, and somehow she'd managed to lower her guard sufficiently for it to hurt all over again. She bit her lip, lowering the generous sweep of dark gold lashes over her eyes to hide her pain.

Dessert was slices of fresh mango with coconut ice-cream.

'Compliments to your chef,' she said at last, sipping her last glassful of red wine, and feeling a hazy, heady sleepiness coming over her, 'but I think jet lag's catching up with me. Or it could be the wine?'

'More likely the Ron Sour.' Luc tilted a teasing eyebrow, examining her soporific smile. 'They pack a hidden punch. Come and dance. That should wake you up.'

The pulsating, syncopated rhythm of the *merengue* music had already lured several couples on to the floor, and the girls from the band were dancing a sensual, hip-jerking, sideways-gyrating dance with the two men, one hand lifted above their heads, flamenco style, but their bodies in close contact from the hips downwards. It all looked rather daunting to Verity. And the thought of doing *that* particular dance with Luc García tied her stomach in knots and sent a rush of blood to the surface of her skin, all over her body...

She stood up and swayed slightly.

'I think I might walk along the beach a little way, first. I don't want to keel over on the dance-floor and embarrass you!'

'I'll come with you,' Luc said easily, sauntering beside her without waiting for any response.

The breeze off the ocean was stronger tonight, rustling the long fronds of the royal palms. Surf rolled in and crashed on to the sand. An enormous spherical moon silvered the sea and beach and palms to a uniform ghostly monochrome.

'I'd better take these shoes off.' She laughed slightly, wobbling on the unsuitable high heels. 'I told Sara they'd be useless for walking on sand!'

She bent to slip off the strappy gold sandals, and lost her balance. Luc fielded her neatly, and then slowly circled her bare upper arms with his fingers and drew her up into his arms.

'Sara was right,' he murmured expressionlessly, his face above her difficult to read, all dark shadows and moonlit angles as she glared up at him.

Every cell in her body seemed to be activated.

'Let me go, Luc!'

'In a minute,' he taunted softly. 'I'm still intrigued by the way you tremble so *indifferently* whenever I touch you...'

'Don't be ridiculous...' With a choked gasp, she felt his hands moving possessively along the slender lines of her arms, then splaying against her back, his arms moving with steely insistence to enfold her completely. The heat which crept stealthily between them at this blatant, inescapable body contact emptied her brain of logical protest.

Trembling, her knees dissolving, she reached up her hands to cling to his shoulders, then closed her eyes in a kind of exultant despair as he bent his head to brush his mouth over her parted lips.

But he moved his mouth away slightly, and her eyes flew open to see a twist of amused mockery on the wide, hard mouth. Her stomach cramped with blind anger. She was longing for Luc to kiss her, that was the stark truth. There was a throb of desire warming her whole body, her breasts felt shivery and sensitive, the nipples traitorously taut beneath the fine fabric of her dress. Luc must be able to feel them through his silk evening shirt. Her pelvis fitted with dangerous ease against him ... her stomach and thighs were on fire ... what was happening to her? How could she have been on the point of marrying Edward, a year ago, yet never before or since have experienced even a quarter of this wrenching, terrifying urgency to surrender body and soul?

The fact that Luc seemed to have the ability to rein in his own desire in this coldly mocking way did nothing for her self-esteem ...

'How is Sara?' he breathed against her cheek, his ability to make mundane conversation while she was feeling so physically devastated making the experience doubly humiliating.

'Sara...she's fine...' Verity managed to croak, hating Luc in that moment more than she'd thought it possible to hate anyone. 'She...she was remarkably cheerful when I left,' she ploughed on, steeling herself against the insidious sensations coursing through her. Shame at her own vulnerability strengthened her resolve, and she tensed and strained away from Luc's overpowering nearness, finishing up with passable self-control, 'Considering she's holding the fort while I take a luxury holiday in the Caribbean...'

'Guilt again?' he murmured, his voice slightly thicker, tightening his hold on her. 'Make a birthday promise to yourself, Verity. Stop feeling guilty. Accept what's on offer, go with the flow.'

She shivered and struggled abruptly in his arms, desperate to get away, but her struggles only succeeded in escalating the heat building between them.

'Luc, please let me go...' she whispered huskily, but in response he only grinned, his teeth flashing very white against the darkness of his face. Then the amusement faded, with a sudden, hungry abruptness, and he crushed her harder against him, seeking her mouth with his and running his tongue enticingly around the circle of her parted lips before deepening the kiss to a hot, intense assault which demolished resistance.

One of the fine gold straps of her dress had slipped off her shoulder, and, with a sensation that the world was spinning out of control around her, Verity felt Luc's cool fingers tracing the sensitive indent of her spine, from base to nape, then stroking down over her shoulders, pushing both straps aside so that the delicate fabric of the dress fell away, leaving her naked to the waist.

'Delectable,' he teased softly, easing her away slightly, his lidded gaze moving hungrily over the firm, high jut of her breasts, bringing a fresh flood of heat to her skin.

Shivering uncontrollably, Verity felt her defences slowly, remorselessly crumbling. It was as if he were touching her with his eyes. Her blood was pounding through her veins. She gasped frantically for air as he lowered his mouth to the full rounded curves of her breasts, and circled each tight, hard pinky-brown nipple with his tongue in tantalising slow motion.

'You taste delectable too, like ripe nectarine...'

'Luc!' It was a choked moan of horror at the deluge of desire his husky words invoked, with the intimacy of what he was doing to her. His fingers were tracing where his tongue had been, his thumbs smoothing the rigid nubs of her nipples, his hands cupping the silken weight of her breasts with increasing insistence.

'Luc, *please* ...!' Terrified of her own wild pleasure, Verity found herself writhing with renewed force. She began to struggle in earnest, half sobbing in the welter of emotions engulfing her.

Then, abruptly, she was free. She twisted away, almost stumbling into the sand, her knees were so weak, wrapping her arms defensively around herself as she fumbled in an agony of humiliation with the bodice of her dress, which seemed to have developed a life of its own.

After an endless few seconds, she jumped nervously as Luc's hard fingers took her arm, and turned her around to face him again. Carefully, he hooked the shoulder-straps in place, covering her vulnerable nakedness with a swift precision that her own trembling attempts had made such heavy weather of, then gazed down into her wide, alarmed eyes, his own expression shuttered.

There was silence. The only sounds were the soft rip and crash of the waves, and the distant strains of music from the hotel terrace.

'*Lo siento*, Verity,' Luc taunted thickly, as if his own iron control was under some strain, 'I will try even harder in future to remember our agreement.'

'What agreement?' she managed to ask, in a small, trembling voice.

'That we are *indifferent* to each other.'

It was never easy to tell what Luc was thinking or feeling, but now the mocking mask was back in place and the irony of his words needed no clarification.

Deeply ashamed of her treacherous response to him, she swung abruptly away, kicked off her sandals, slung them over her wrist and marched ahead of him back towards the lights of the Hotel Laguna, furiously conscious that with soft, fine sand underfoot it was almost impossible to march with any degree of dignity.

Pablito greeted them with a wave as they stepped back on to the terrace.

'Telephone for you, Señor García...'

Luc cursed under his breath.

'Tell them I'm not available,' he reminded the waiter, ushering Verity back into her seat at their table. The last thing she wanted to do was sit down with Luc again, but she felt so swamped by conflicting emotions, and so annihilated by the desire he'd aroused inside her, that she felt momentarily beyond argument. Drawing slow, steadying breaths, she battled with her composure, hoping that she didn't look as wildly dishevelled as she felt.

'And bring us more coffee, Pablito,' Luc added, glancing at her flushed, dismayed face with a wry gleam in his eyes.

'The telephone call is urgent, *señor.*'

Luc's dark brows drew together in a frown.

'Who is it?'

'Señor de Santana.'

Verity felt some of her fighting spirit returning to her rescue, as she watched the expression fade from Luc's face. Still smarting from the humiliating episode on the beach, she cut in quickly, 'Santana? Isn't that your *wife's* maiden name? Juliette de Santana, wasn't it?'

'My ex-wife,' Luc corrected grimly, his eyes narrowing on her bland expression. 'Federico de Santana is my father-in-law.'

'You'd better go and speak to him, hadn't you?' she suggested helpfully, eyes wide in mock innocence.

With an unrepeatable curse under his breath, Luc swung away, and strode towards the bar, and Verity sat watching the band and the dancers, yet hardly seeing them. She ought to make a bolt for the villa, but she felt temporarily paralysed, drained of energy. The memory of Luc's mouth and fingers was still scorching her breasts, beneath the lamentably flimsy material of her dress. Her stomach was still hollow with suppressed longing. But why on earth should she now feel so doubly churned up inside? She wasn't sure which was the more unsettling—her involuntary reaction to Luc's sensual assault on the beach, or the reminder of his past marriage intruding on the traumas of the evening . . .

But she felt illogical tears sting her eyelids as she stared blindly at the band. She was feeling helplessly angry and hurt and utterly confused by her own emotions, when a laughing male voice spoke behind her.

'Verity! Surprise, surprise!'

The voice was familiar, yet alien.

Startled, hardly believing her ears, she spun round to see Elliot Grosvenor standing there, resplendent in a white tropical suit and with a spray of pink hibiscus in his top buttonhole, a bottle of champagne in one hand and a pink-wrapped present in the other.

'Elliot!' Nonplussed, she could only gape at him in open-mouthed shock. '*Elliot*? What on earth are *you* doing here?'

'We had a date, didn't we?' he complained comically, fishing a handkerchief out of his pocket and mopping his forehead, before sitting down at the chair beside her. 'So here I am, a couple of thousand pounds poorer, a little late for dinner, but still in time to wish you a very happy birthday, Verity, darling!'

CHAPTER FOUR

'I JUST can't believe you actually followed me out here, Elliot!' Verity was so pole-axed that she wasn't sure quite how she felt. Angry, mainly. Angry, and baffled. Poor Sara! She must have rung to tell him where Verity was going, and Elliot had apparently jotted down the address and hailed a passing aeroplane...

This was ridiculous. What on earth did Elliot see in her, anyway? Whenever she looked in a mirror, she saw an ordinary face, oval and rather too long, plain hazel eyes and plain hazel hair, a freckled snub nose which didn't even approach the term 'classical', and an over-large mouth which looked terrible with lipstick on...and as for her figure, well, she wasn't overweight, and her curves were in the right places, but Hollywood glamour-girl she was not. Elliot was the one with the matinée-idol looks. With his smooth golden hair and smooth golden tan, and his air of moneyed indolence, he reminded her of a 1930s film star. And he was always so insufferably pleased with himself; she found it hard to see what Sara found so irresistible in the man...

Raking her tousled curls back from her forehead, she gazed blankly at the self-satisfied smile on Elliot's face, and shook her head.

'Are you booked in to this hotel?'

'Yup! I checked it out with the travel operators. They seemed to rate it reasonably highly. Though I doubt if there's anywhere on this poverty-stricken island which matches up to my normal standards...'

'No?' She found herself smarting indignantly. She'd only been here a day, and she was mentally jumping to the island's defence. 'This is a beautiful place, though! The people are wonderful, warm and friendly. And there's just about everything here—mountains, rivers, waterfalls, miles of unspoilt beaches...'

'You sound like a travelogue, sweetheart. I've seen it all before. All these Third-World Caribbean islands are the same. It's you I've come to see!'

'Well, you've wasted your time and money, I'm afraid! Didn't Sara tell you I'd be *working*?' she retorted bluntly.

'Looks like a pretty cushy job to me!' Elliot grinned at her, his pale blue eyes moving appreciatively over her appearance in the filmy dress. 'Lord, Verity, I wish you'd drop this ice-queen act of yours. Seeing you in that dress makes my temperature rise more than this blasted humidity!'

'It's not an ice-queen act! This is the way I am, Elliot. If you don't like it, it's a pity you've wasted all this money following me out here, uninvited!'

'I do like it! I adore it, sweetheart. I love my women unattainable!'

With a despairing groan, she shook her head and laughed.

'It's hopeless! You must be...*blinkered* or something! The world is full of females who must think you're the best thing since seedless grapes, and you have to chase after me! I am not interested, Elliot! So why?'

'Ever since I tasted your spinach roulade, Verity, I knew we must be made for each other!' Elliot leered suggestively at her, and she burst out laughing. At least occasional flashes of humour saved him from being totally obnoxious. Maybe Sara wasn't quite so blind after all...

'That's a superb-looking necklace you're wearing!' Elliot was saying, leaning closer to inspect the pendant. 'The real thing, definitely not paste! Business *must* be good, darling.'

'I...it was a birthday present,' she said quietly, glancing over at the bar, where she could see Luc still on the telephone. His gaze was levelled broodingly on the scene at their table, as she smiled and talked with Elliot. She felt her pulse-rate jolt and speed up, and the palms of her hands suddenly felt slightly damp with a surge of defiant anger. How dared Luc watch her in that hawk-like fashion, as if he owned her or something? 'It's amber,' she added, distractedly. 'A stone they mine here, in the mountains...'

'It may be amber, but set in twenty-four-carat gold and real diamonds. The colour suits you. Goes with your eyes...but you haven't opened *my* present!' Elliot was complaining, pushing a pink-wrapped package towards her. She caught her breath, then tore her eyes from Luc's dark gaze and smiled blandly at Elliot.

'No. And I'm not going to! Take it back to London and give it to Sara.'

'But it's Chanel No. 5...'

'Can't stand it. Sara loves it. Let's dance—this crazy thing they're doing on the dance-floor looks fun!'

Jumping up, she towed Elliot into the mass of gyrating bodies, and they tried to ape the complicated, hip-swaying technique, with conspicuous lack of success.

'Maybe this wasn't such a good idea,' she gasped in fits of laughter, as Elliot trod on her toes for the tenth time, and he showed signs of rebellion by drawing her into a classic 'smooch' instead.

'Darned if I can get the hang of the rhythm,' Elliot was complaining, perspiration beading his forehead and upper lip. 'Frankly, sweetheart, I'd rather go and lie down somewhere...'

'No chance!' she shot back sweetly, the smile fading from her face as she saw Luc appear suddenly behind them, his dark features cool, a dangerous glitter in his eyes.

'Luc,' she began brightly, 'this is Elliot, a friend of mine from London... Elliot, this is Luc García...my—er—the owner of the hotel.'

'Good to meet you, Elliot.' Luc's acid rasp blatantly implied the reverse. 'Allow me to teach the lady how to dance the *merengue*,' he added, levering Elliot aside with what looked to be a distinctly unsubtle thrust, and hauling Verity into the uncompromising hardness of his arms.

The blood seemed to surge in her veins at the movement of their bodies, close together.

'That wasn't very polite, Luc...' she began huskily, but the words dried in her throat at the harsh brilliance of the gaze turned down on her.

'*Merengue* is not a very polite dance,' he mocked, guiding her expertly in a series of primitive movements which felt almost as explicit as publicly making love. Verity could feel her skin burning all over her body. 'Put your hand here, like this...' he instructed, placing her fingers against the sleek muscle of his shoulder. 'And the other arm up in the air...like so...'

His own hand pressed firmly in the small of her back, bringing her hips and thighs into relentless contact with his. The fast, syncopated saxophone music, the irresistibly Caribbean beat, washed over them and around them, threatening to totally swamp her senses.

'I didn't mean the dance,' she snapped shakily, wondering how much more of this she could take, 'I meant your attitude towards Elliot.'

'Elliot?' he grated, his voice ominously soft. 'Who the hell is Elliot, anyway?'

'I told you...he's a friend from London.'

'Did you know he was coming?'

'No...but would it matter if I had?' She scanned Luc's sardonic face indignantly. 'He is paying his own flight and accommodation, you know! He's perfectly entitled to act of his own free will!'

'Are you lovers?'

Verity's face felt crimson.

'That's none of your business!'

Luc's face hardened, his eyes very bright beneath the heavy lids.

'No? After the way you acted just now on the beach, *cara*, I feel entitled to ask. How do you like our *merengue* rhythm, Verity?'

The husky purr in his voice was the last straw, the insistent pressure of Luc's body against hers suddenly unbearable. Her composure deserted her.

'I don't,' she snapped furiously. 'I feel as if I'm being mauled by an animal! *Excuse* me!'

She wrenched herself from his arms and began to half walk, half run from the dance-floor, her only conscious destination the safe haven of her villa. She caught a fleeting glimpse of Elliot, sitting drinking a large brandy and looking visibly pained, at the table on the terrace. She was rude to march off without saying goodnight, but she felt in no fit state to talk to him or anyone else now...never mind Elliot, he could think what he liked...

She stumbled through the palms, and with a half-sob she began to run, desperate to put as much space between herself and Luc as she could, her high heels sinking into the soft, sandy ground, impeding her progress. Now she knew why she normally shunned this kind of footwear. Teetering high heels made her *feel* more vulnerable, and physically hindered her ability to escape situations she didn't like...

She reached the villa terrace and felt the heel on one gold sandal collapse underneath her foot, jarring her ankle and knocking her off balance. Grabbing the wooden railing for support, she gasped in frustration as her knees threatened to buckle beneath her.

'*Blast* these stupid sandals!' she sobbed impotently, collapsing on to the wooden steps leading up to the terrace and wrenching them from her feet, hurling them furiously on to the ground and massaging her sore ankle.

Luc appeared just in time to witness the outburst. He stopped, silently assessing the scene. His expression deadpan, he came to retrieve the gold shoes, and turned them slowly over in his hands to inspect the broken heel.

'There was no need to run away, Verity,' he said slowly, a thoughtful note in his voice. 'You have no need to be frightened of me...'

'Just give me my shoes, and leave me alone!'

'They're useless, I'm afraid.'

'Good. I hate them. I never want to wear the wretched things again!'

He raised a slanted brow.

'Why did you wear them tonight?'

'Heaven knows!' she snapped, wincing as her ankle throbbed more persistently. 'From now on I shall stick to trainers!'

'I doubt if trainers would look quite as effective with that particular dress,' Luc pointed out, with a wry half-smile. 'Have you hurt your ankle?'

'No, I'm fine. Would you please go away, and leave me alone?'

'Certainly. When I see that you can walk safely into the villa.'

'Oh, for the love of...' She hauled herself upright, trembling with annoyance, and began to march up the steps, but when she put down her left foot she couldn't smother her sharp intake of breath.

'Stop playing the stubborn martyr,' Luc suggested easily, coming to slide his arm round her waist, taking her weight as he led her inside, flicking on the wall-lights at the door. 'Your ankle is twisted. It will need bandaging.'

'Luc, I do not need your help, so...'

'Look, it's already swelling.' He'd guided her to the rattan sofa, pushed her none too gently on to the down-filled green floral seat-cushions, and was squatting effortlessly in front of her, inspecting her ankle with an air of businesslike expertise.

'It's nothing—just a simple twist. I should know, it's my ankle!' she told him impatiently. 'I'll put it in cold water. By morning it'll be fine!'

'I'll ring over to the hotel for the first-aid box,' Luc stated calmly, ignoring her protests. Using the phone briefly, he returned to pull a rattan stool across, propping up her leg, and then examining it with gentle skill.

'Not broken. The Achilles' tendon is still intact. The ligaments may be slightly torn...'

'Rubbish! It would be like a balloon by now if I'd torn any ligaments... oh, please stop!'

The involuntary plea was more in response to the disturbing effect of his fingers on her skin, but Luc frowned in contrition, misunderstanding.

'*Lo siento*, I didn't mean to hurt you. But it's as well to check the injury thoroughly.'

'You boast medical qualifications in your repertoire, do you?' she queried shakily, evading his eyes.

'No... but I've had plenty of experience of sprains and breakages. The polo field can be a rough place...'

He stopped, seeing her face tighten.

'But you already know that,' he added abruptly. Straightening up with the muscular fluidity of the supremely fit, he disappeared into the kitchen and returned with a glass of brandy.

'Here...'

Verity took the glass from his hand, and took a small sip, feeling the fiery spirit trickle down her throat, catching her breath slightly. Her nerves were in far worse shape than her ankle, if the truth were known. But the brandy had a calming, anaesthetic effect.

Maria, the hotel receptionist, appeared at the patio doors with the first-aid box, and came in full of sympathy, unearthing bandages and lint and witch-hazel and proceeding to strap up Verity's ankle with speedy efficiency, before Verity could convince her it wasn't necessary.

'You should see how it feels tomorrow,' she advised with a friendly smile, her eyes switching from Luc's watchful presence to Verity's wary tension as she retreated with her box. 'We can call in the doctor if necessary, can't we, Señor García?'

'Of course. Thank you, Maria.'

Luc received another of Maria's eager smiles in farewell, and Verity suppressed a stab of bitter humour. Another besotted acolyte for Luc's collection? She wouldn't have been surprised to see the girl blow him a kiss.

'How is your *wife*, Luc?' she queried abruptly, thinking of the phone call earlier and unable to resist the urge to goad Luc the way he so frequently goaded her. Perhaps the brandy supplied the Dutch courage. Her resolve flinched at the chilling expression she saw in Luc's intent blue gaze.

'My *ex*-wife. As well as can be expected,' he retorted drily. 'I think that is the usual expression?'

'Is it?' Verity took another mouthful of brandy, and eased her leg slightly on the stool. 'Is that what your *ex*-father-in-law rang to tell you earlier?'

The blue gaze narrowed intently.

'Why this sudden interest, Verity?'

'Why not?' she countered blithely, attempting to wriggle her toes and registering only a minor degree of pain. 'Or do you feel I'm invading your *privacy*, by any chance? The way *you* did when you had the nerve to ask about my relationship with Elliot Grosvenor?'

There was a short, charged silence. Luc turned and strolled to the kitchen, returning with a glass of brandy for himself. He sat down in a nearby chair, an ominous gleam in his eyes.

'So that's his name. Grosvenor. I've heard it.'

'I expect you have. His family own merchant banks. He moves in the wealthy circles you seem to be so well up in!'

'The man's a creep. How the hell did you manage to get involved with him?'

Colour flared involuntarily to her face, but through anger rather than embarrassment.

'Elliot might have rather more money than he knows what to do with, but he is not a creep,' she stated icily. 'He's an incredibly successful City futures dealer.'

'Enough said.'

Their eyes locked, molten gold with mocking dark blue. Verity shifted abruptly on the sofa, suddenly aware of her vulnerable state, the fine soft fabric of her dress far too revealing for her peace of mind. A thin gold strap had fallen down one shoulder, and she quickly hooked it back, drawing her knees together in unconscious defence. The twist on Luc's mouth told her he was well aware of her discomfort.

'Don't worry, I'm not about to leap on you like an animal,' he advised her drily, 'despite your flattering comments on the dance-floor.'

'Thank you!' She lowered her eyes to hide her wave of reaction.

'I wonder what prompts our choices of career?' he went on musingly, his expression unfathomable. 'There's Grosvenor, content to spend his time wheeling and dealing in millions of pounds of other people's money. And then there's you, hooked on cooking food for a living...'

'Well, go on?' she taunted softly. 'What about you? Spending your life on horseback, whacking a ball around a field and risking death or injury every time you do it? The prime case for a psychiatrist's couch!'

'It's the acceptable modern equivalent to thundering around with a sabre, chopping off the enemy's head. Or so I've heard.'

'Sounds absolutely disgusting,' Verity retorted coldly. Trust Luc García to have some macho, ultra-masculine view. 'So what do *you* get out of it? Do you often feel you want to chop off the enemy's head?'

Luc shrugged lightly, his mouth twisting in amusement.

'Fortunately, the rules of the game aim to prevent such undesirable excesses, Verity. I grew up on a horse-breeding ranch in South America, where polo is a way of life. I have ridden all my life. I've always enjoyed team sports. Polo is a good blend of the two.'

'I think Edward saw it differently,' Verity said slowly, sipping the brandy again. It had seemed a very long day. After the variety of emotions triggered this evening, she was feeling slightly shell-shocked.

'Did he?'

Verity caught the quizzical gleam in Luc's eyes. It didn't surprise her that Luc seemed unaware of Edward's motivations for playing the game he so blithely took for granted. Luc didn't strike her as the intuitive type. And men didn't confide in each other, did they? Except briefly, perhaps...in moments of acute stress...

'I think he saw polo as his way of gaining social acceptance. He was the first of his family to go to public school, and playing polo professionally was his way of proving a point—getting even, if you like, with people he felt might have looked down on him...'

'It's an interesting theory...how's the ankle feeling?' Without waiting for her reply, Luc stood up and fetched the brandy bottle, taking her glass and pouring another measure before she'd had a chance to refuse. She watched him angrily as he splashed more of the strong spirit into his own glass, and sat down again with that intent, watchful expression on his face.

'My ankle is feeling fine! And what do you mean by "an interesting theory"? I ought to know what made Edward tick, I was going to marry him, after all!'

There was a short silence.

'Ah, yes. So you were. Why, Verity?'

The question caught her off-guard.

'Why? Why what?'

'Why were you going to marry Edward? What was it that attracted you to him?'

She was floundering, she realised, sensing Luc's cynical appraisal as she sought for an answer.

'He was kind, gentle, dependable...'

'So is a faithful dog. Is that all?'

Colour surged to her face at the scathing tone in Luc's voice. Replacing her glass very carefully on the glass-topped cane table near by, she pushed a shaky hand through her hair, and levelled a defiant stare at Luc's infuriatingly nonchalant gaze.

'I don't have to explain, or justify, or confide anything to you...!' she began in a low voice, but Luc was shaking his head mockingly.

'Why so defensive, I wonder? The answer to the question should have been very straightforward. Unless you have something to hide, something you are ashamed of?'

'Stop it, Luc! I'm not sure what you're trying to prove, but the truth is that Edward and I had a close, loving relationship, we had plenty in common, we shared the same ideals about marriage...'

'What ideals?'

'That marriage is for keeps! Something you stick with, and work at. Most males look for some glamorous accessory they can swap for a newer model. Females tend to look for more enduring characteristics...security...'

'Not all females, Verity.' There was a warning softness in Luc's voice, and she crossed her arms angrily across her breasts, sensing the nature of his attack and longing to wipe that knowing smile off his face. 'And I submit that you wanted a secure, undemanding base from which to conduct your exciting little sexual adventures?'

'*What*?' The colour drained from her face, and then surged back as the icy indictment sank in. 'Luc, how dare you say that? Just because——'

'Just because I have evidence to back up the allegation?' he shot back ruthlessly, his eyes darkening. 'What a shame I am not like Edward, Verity. Kind, gentle, dependable—and gullible?'

'I know how it might have seemed, that night,' she countered unsteadily, anger and guilt warring for supremacy, 'but, believe me, it was a total aberration... it had never happened before, and it would never, ever have happened again! I was totally committed to Edward! We would have had a happy marriage. I would have been totally faithful, and he would never have let me down——'

'It sounds very convenient. A very prosaic recipe for a prospective husband. All this security and safety and dependability... at the expense of love? At the expense of passion?' The soft gibe cut in on her sentence.

'You're wrong!' she countered, suppressing her temper with the very limits of her self-control. 'It's not prosaic to want security! And I did love Edward!'

'No. You did not love Edward. If you had, you would never have responded to me the way you did that night on the terrace of the polo club in Florida,' Luc asserted quietly.

'Luc, that's a *foul* thing to suggest! And you're a fine one to talk about love! What about the way you treated your wife?' she said in a choked voice.

There was a resounding silence, in which other noises seemed to grow disproportionately louder. The hum of the ceiling fan, the shrill of the cicadas, the distant strains of the *merengue* band blending with the hiss and suck of the ocean just beyond the terrace.

'My *ex*-wife,' he said at last. His tone had altered slightly, become ominously quiet, but it was impossible to decipher his real thoughts. 'And what do you know about my marriage, Verity? Who have you talked to about it? Edward?'

Verity shook her head. 'No. It wasn't Edward.'

'Then who?' There was an icy glint in Luc's eyes.

She shrugged uneasily, and tentatively lowered her sore ankle to the floor, wincing as her weight put a strain on it. She'd be perfectly able to hobble, but not to stalk away with any dignity. A wave of frustration washed over her. Blast those gold sandals! Pride kept her trapped here, in the softly lit sitting-room of the villa. She had the sensation of being subtly imprisoned with an interrogator...

'I can't remember. Someone in Florida last year. Does it matter, for heaven's sake?'

'It matters because I should like to know in what way I am rumoured to have ill-treated my ex-wife.'

'I suppose you'd deny it all if you could! But frankly I found it all too likely! Your wife became ill, didn't she?'

Luc's blue gaze had narrowed to slits of brilliant light. Verity swallowed convulsively but ploughed on.

'Too ill to be much good as a wife any more, I gather? So you divorced her, and then *very* generously offered to pay for her nursing home expenses! So forget the marriage vows, "in sickness and in health"? Much too inconvenient, I presume? Off with the old, and on with the new, which you've been pursuing with maximum publicity ever since! Can you deny *that*?'

The colour seemed to recede slightly from the swarthy darkness of his face, and the expression on the rugged features was suddenly so coldly menacing that Verity was overcome with relief when the sound of Elliot's voice interrupted them.

'Verity! I asked in the hotel, and they said I'd find you here!' Elliot came to the open patio doors and stared in at the tense scene, his expression indignant. 'You might have said something before rushing off like that! Lord above, I fly all the way out here to see you, and you behave as if nothing's happened . . .'

He frowned, suddenly spotting the bandage on her ankle.

'I say, what's happened to your leg? Did this happen dancing that blasted Caribbean dance with this character?'

He glanced dismissively towards Luc, who had risen slowly from his chair with controlled precision to tower a good four inches above Elliot. The shadow of a smile on his mouth was far from humorous. Elliot's smug expression faded.

'I'd say Verity was in greater danger of physical injury while dancing with you, Grosvenor. You're in this villa uninvited. I advise you to leave.'

'I *beg* your pardon?' Elliot was staring at Luc, his pale eyes almost popping out of his head in an outrage Verity might have found comical in other circumstances.

'Elliot, not now...' she began wearily, levering herself to her feet and supporting her weight on the sofa-back. 'We'll talk tomorrow.'

'Just hang on a minute.' He was switching his eyes rapidly from Verity's flushed cheeks to Luc's masklike calm, his own colour rising. 'Is there something going on between you two?'

'No, there's nothing going on between us, and frankly Elliot——'

'You heard the lady,' Luc cut across her words, his deep voice coldly incisive. 'So either find yourself some other holiday entertainment, or find another hotel!'

'Well, really,' blustered Elliot, 'I've never been so insulted...'

The guiding hand which steered Elliot back out of the villa looked none too gentle, and Verity was rigid with indignation when Luc returned a few seconds later, apparently unruffled, a gleam of unholy amusement on his dark face.

'Your friend has succumbed to the rigours of jet lag,' he drawled negligently, sweeping a disturbingly brilliant gaze over her as she clenched her hands in impotent fury.

'I suppose you think it's highly amusing, being downright rude to one of my friends? Or is this how you *normally* treat guests at your hotel?' she began hotly.

'Get rid of him, Verity,' Luc ordered curtly, his amusement abruptly vanishing. He projected an air of such controlled menace that she had to summon all her failing courage to stand up to him. Dark and brooding, in the restrained elegance of his beige dinner-jacket, he radiated cool authority, very much in charge, infuriatingly so...

'Stop ordering me around!' she said on a rising note of indignation. 'Both Elliot and I are over twenty-one, free citizens of the UK, and entitled to do as we please... so why don't you just go off to Argentina, and play polo, and——'

The glitter of cold contempt in his eyes was so intense, she stopped abruptly.

'And what?' he jeered with soft disdain. 'Leave you to make a fool of Elliot Grosvenor, the way you would have made a fool of Edward?'

She stared at him, aghast.

'How can you say that?' she said chokingly, hardly believing her ears.

'I can say it quite easily. Just as you can brand me a callous, ruthless deserter of my sick wife. *Basta*! Enough! Go to bed, Verity,' he grated savagely, with the air of having reached the outer boundaries of his patience. 'We can resume our *interesting* conversation some other time...'

'*What* interesting conversation?' she whispered, shaking with anger.

'The one your friend Grosvenor interrupted. You were telling me how I discarded my wife for a healthier model? I'd be fascinated to hear more. Another time. But not now. Tonight, I would not trust my self-control sufficiently to hear any more of your allegations!'

The ruthless twist of his mouth bore no resemblance to a smile as he turned abruptly and strode out of the villa.

CHAPTER FIVE

VERITY stayed motionless, staring at the doorway for a long time after Luc had disappeared, her emotions in chaos. She felt paralysed with misery and confusion. She longed to dive under a cool shower, drown her agitation in soothing jets of water, but the bandage on her ankle was a handicap. So was walking, she discovered, grimly hobbling across the room and into her bedroom, which the maids had cleaned and tidied to perfection in her absence.

Finally perfecting an uneven limp, she went through the routine of washing and teeth-cleaning with mechanical preoccupation and then crawled on to her bed to lie there, face up in the darkness, the day's events replaying in her head with relentless clarity, heavily overshadowed by tonight's shattering scene with Luc...

Elliot's appearance had been a shock. After all her secret hopes of matchmaking between him and Sara, it seemed positively indecent of him to pop up out of the blue like this, trying to pursue a relationship which didn't exist.

But Elliot's involvement paled into obscurity beside the bitter exchange with Luc tonight...

She'd never grasped how deeply he despised her. She still found it hard to accept. The guilt over that mindless aberration last year was bad enough. But knowing that Luc García was standing in judgement over her...

Verity shuddered, and rolled on to her side, ignoring the distant throb from her ankle. It felt less painful already. By tomorrow it would be tolerable to limp on. She refused to be laid up by something so ridiculous.

A decision swam into her mind, and she resolved to act on it. First thing in the morning, she'd contact the airport and book her flight home. Pointless staying here any longer. Luc had brought her here for some kind of refined revenge for her behaviour in Florida. The 'obligation' to Edward, the talk of relaxation, was just a pretence... Luc was a sadist. She doubted if he even *liked* women. Look at how he'd treated his wife!

Luc could find someone else to torment. And Elliot could do as he pleased. She was past caring...

Blanking her mind to the disturbing images of the episode on the beach, and the chilling expression in Luc's eyes when he'd left her tonight, she fell abruptly into a deep, dreamless sleep.

The ringing of the telephone was the first thing she heard as she woke. She propped herself up on one arm, fumbling sleepily for the receiver beside the bed.

Sara's voice came over the thousands of miles of line as clear and strong as if she were phoning from the next town.

'Sara—how lovely to hear your voice!' Sleepily, Verity realised how much she meant it. A wave of home-sickness engulfed her. What was she *doing* over here, being hustled and harassed and verbally abused by a man she hardly knew and had never even liked?

'I hope it's not too early over there?' Sara sounded either agitated or excited, Verity decided, as she blearily checked her watch and realised it was only six a.m. Caribbean time.

'It's not *quite* the middle of the night,' she assured her friend wryly, smothering a yawn, and adding with a touch of concern, 'What is it, Sara? Not a problem with the business?'

'Far from it!' Sara laughed delightedly. 'Which would you like first? The good news, or the even better news?'

'Er—I'll start with the good news.' Verity was sitting up straight now, pushing handfuls of wayward honey-gold curls from her eyes and wriggling the toes on her injured foot with a fresh surge of optimism.

'You remember we were doing that catering for the North Downs Polo Club charity match, in May?'

Verity felt the smile freeze on her lips. North Downs was the club Luc frequented when he was in England for the season. Luc's influence again. Was he hoping to strangle her with sinister benevolence?

'Verity? Are you still there?'

'Yes. I'm still here. And yes, I remember. We're supposed to be on approval? If we get it right, we stand to gain more business from them?'

'Right. Well, two of the club committee members were at another of our dinners recently, and apparently they were so impressed that, rather than wait to see how the first event goes down, they've just confirmed they're giving us the contract for the rest of their sponsored events this season!'

Verity was frowning fiercely into space.

'Sounds wonderful... what does that mean, exactly?' She was playing for time, fighting with her temper.

'Well, you know—they have various companies, like prestige car manufacturers, wine-importers, who sponsor polo matches to promote their products. They pay for the whole thing, all the guests, the hire of the marquee, and everything, but North Downs Polo Club are going to stipulate that *we* do the food!'

'It sounds too good to be true...won't the previous caterers mind?'

'All's fair in love and catering franchises! Don't worry, it's all completely above-board. So kindly give your gorgeous Luc García a great big kiss for me, will you, darling? On the strength of it, I've just booked myself a long-haul trip to Australia and Singapore! You'll be able to spare me by the end of August. I can see Tom and Trina's baby before he grows into a little boy!'

Tom was Sara's brother, Verity remembered, her stomach twisting itself into painful knots as she reviewed her current plans. Sara sounded so thrilled, so full of optimism for the huge success of their business. And on the face of it, why not? They both worked hard, and were both talented cooks. And with Luc García's relentless, behind-the-scenes string-pulling, it seemed as if they could do no wrong, as if business would eternally fall into their laps regardless of considerable rival competition in the catering industry...

It was an unreal situation, but presumably all she had to do was stay on reasonable terms with Luc García and the situation would continue? Was that the way it was? Were her previous hints at paranoia justified? Was this some sort of outlandish *blackmail*, after all?

'You don't seem terribly pleased!' Sara was protesting, and Verity made an effort to collect her wits.

'Sorry—it *is* rather early in the morning, Sara. It all sounds marvellous...'

'And how's your working holiday going? I'll bet you're having some fun as well, aren't you?'

'Oh, loads of fun,' Verity agreed expressionlessly. 'I'll tell you all about it when I get back. Save our phone bill, Sara; you never know when we might need to cut our overheads! See you soon—take care...'

When the line went dead, she sat motionless in bed, absently clutching the receiver, torn between consideration for Sara and the overpowering urge to escape from Luc.

When Maria's voice on Reception suddenly spoke over the line, she realised she'd been holding the receiver off the hook, and quickly apologised, replacing it with a slightly shaking hand.

What was she to do? A wave of despairing indecision came over her. How would it look to Sara if she alienated Luc, and jeopardised all their extra business? And she hadn't had the heart to mention Elliot's presence here. Sara would probably find out, but not through Verity. Goodness knew why Sara was so besotted with Elliot, but Verity certainly wasn't going to do anything to obstruct the ultimate course of true love, if she could help it...

She needed another twenty-four hours to think things through, she concluded finally. Above all, she mustn't let her own murky collection of guilt and anger over Edward and Luc cloud the issue, and unfairly affect her friend's share of their business...

An early swim seemed an attractive option. Determinedly she unwound the bandage from her ankle, and inspected the damage. A faint blue and yellow bruise was beginning to emerge, but it wasn't swollen, and when she gingerly put her weight on it the pain was quite bearable. The salt-water would be therapeutic.

Confronting the mirror as she slipped into a black and white striped swimsuit, she realised with a jolt that she was still wearing the pendant Luc had given her for her birthday.

It glittered richly against her skin. Her heart contracted when she recalled Elliot's words—real diamonds? Solid gold? Why would Luc lavish such expensive jewellery on her, when he so clearly despised her? It didn't make sense. Nothing made sense any more.

Automatically, she reached to unfasten it, and dropped it with nerveless fingers on to the dressing-table. She'd rather die than accept it from him. She'd find the right moment to give it back to him. Maybe by post, she reflected, grimacing at her lamentable cowardice...

A few minutes later she was wading into the surf, breathing in the heady scents on the trade winds, her eyes half closed on the warm, misty horizon. With a jolt of self-knowledge, as she sank forwards into the warm Caribbean waters, she realised that leaving here was the very last thing she wanted to do. If it weren't for the tension and bitterness associated with Luc, she doubted if she'd *ever* want to leave this idyllic place...

Turning to float on her back, bobbing over the waves, she gazed back up the white crescent of deserted sand at the splashes of wildly exotic colour in the bushes dotted among the palm trees. Bright scarlet, vivid orange, sunshine-yellow, lush deep pink. In the early morning glow of the sun, they looked so beautiful that she found herself mesmerised by the scene.

She didn't even know their names, she admitted to herself ruefully, feeling a nostalgic memory stab her unexpectedly. That had always been one of her parents' obsessions—discovering the names of every wild flower they found on country walks. They'd always taken pocket books with them, with the intention of identifying anything they found. Happy times together, the three of them, before the tragic outcome of one of their beloved rock-climbing expeditions, and before Verity had subsequently discovered that her parents' blissfully happy marriage had all been a sham, that all the while her father had been deceiving her mother, deceiving Verity, pretending to be the perfect husband and devoted father while pursuing his own private world which totally excluded them . . .

The memories seemed to squeeze her heart suddenly, and she flipped over and began to swim slowly out to sea, her eyes on the coral reef she'd snorkelled around with Luc yesterday.

She didn't want to think about her father, about how deeply she'd been hurt by that discovery. Live for the moment, she reminded herself philosophically. She focused instead on the miraculous tropical beauty surrounding her, switching her thoughts into a more positive gear.

How could she think of flying back to the cool greyness of London this morning, when she hadn't even discovered what those flowers around the beach were called?

'Verity!' It was Luc's voice. She turned and watched him slice effortlessly through the water towards her, keeping her expression carefully neutral as he reached her.

'Good morning, Luc.'

'What the devil are you doing?'

'Swimming?' she suggested mildly. 'Why? Did I miss a shark warning, or something?'

'I can see that you're swimming. Why are you nearly two hundred yards from the shore, with a sprained ankle? Are you trying to drown yourself?'

'Not at all. My ankle is feeling much better. I told you it was a mild twist, when you were making all that ridiculous fuss last night!'

Luc thrust black hair from his forehead, glaring at her so furiously that she felt her lips twitch, in spite of everything.

'Stop looking at me like that!' she exclaimed, beginning to swim again, slowly heading for the shore at a sedate breast-stroke. Her ankle had started to ache a little, but she'd rather drown than admit that to Luc. 'Why were you so worried about my drowning, anyway? Just because you'd be deprived of a victim to torment?'

Luc swore roughly under his breath, his glance shuttered as he swam beside her, pacing himself to a smooth breast-stroke to stay alongside.

'I realise you have me summed up as a cross between Machiavelli and the Marquis de Sade,' he said tersely, 'but my ambition is not to torment you, Verity.'

'Then what is your ambition?' she demanded, spurred by a surge of angry frustration. 'What do you want from me? Sara rang to tell me about the North Downs Polo Club contract. She's so thrilled about all the extra business, she's booked herself a trip to Australia! Frankly, Luc, I'd love to tell you where to stick your polo club contract and your working holiday and all the rest of your power-complex interfering in our affairs, but where will that leave us? Scrabbling around for business because the great Luc García has withdrawn his patronage? We'd have been better off without your interference! We'd have made it on our own reputations, and I wouldn't have to worry about keeping on the right side of someone like you!'

They'd reached the shallows before Luc replied. He watched her climb to her feet, and shovel handfuls of dripping wet hair from her eyes, before he straightened slowly to his full height beside her.

'Is that really what you think of me?' he said softly. 'You think I would attack your business out of spite?'

She opened her mouth to retort, and the words dried in her throat. The electric-blue gaze was so blindingly hypnotic in the rugged darkness of Luc's face that she felt her certainties dissolve into fragments all over again. Her mind went blank. Luc was too close, as they stood there in the sunshine on the white sand, the sea-water running in rivulets down their bodies. She found herself mesmerised by the glisten of the beads of water on the black hairs on his skin, the way they trickled along the contours of hard muscle on his chest, then arrowed in towards the V of dark hair below his navel, disappearing beneath the brief black of his swimming trunks.

'Well?' he persisted, his voice deepening and thickening slightly as he stared at her. 'Is it, Verity?'

'I don't know... I just don't *know*!' It was a choked sob, and she swung away quickly, too quickly for her ankle. Luc grabbed her arm to prevent her from crumpling back down into the shallow water swirling around their feet, and once again she found herself in the ignominious position of quite literally falling into his arms.

But this time the emotional reaction scorching through her body felt infinitely more powerful. Even in the heat of sun, she shivered involuntarily, and with a low groan Luc caught her harder against him. Abruptly she reached her hands up to his shoulders, melting inside with a heat which burned and tormented, caution and suspicion temporarily wiped from her mind. Breast to chest, stomach to stomach, thigh to thigh, they welded together in the flames which threatened to consume them.

'Verity...' He breathed her name on a husky groan, as his hands caressed and moulded every inch of her back, sliding over the wetness of her skin, then smoothed the tangled mane of hair from her cheek, his finger briefly lingering on the trembling curve of her upper lip before he bent his mouth to kiss her.

She shouldn't be letting this happen. Distant caution was flashing warnings, but there was a fog in her brain, confusing her thoughts, letting the physical clamour of her senses rule her actions. Not even a brief, vivid flash of comparison between this hectic desire and that stormy few minutes of illicit passion twelve months ago could extinguish the fire within her.

Gasping softly as Luc's mouth lifted from hers, she gazed up at him with a wave of disbelief, read the blatant hunger in his brilliant blue eyes, and felt her heart beginning to thump audibly against her breastbone.

'*Madre de Dios*!' he breathed hoarsely, his fingers cupping her face, his eyes searching the wide, dazed honey-gold gaze fixed steadily on him. 'Why do I want you so badly? You think I am a vindictive wife-beater, you say you are my victim and that I enjoy tormenting you? And yet I want to make love to you right here, now, on this beach, on the edge of the Atlantic ocean! Are you a witch, Verity? Have you cast a spell on me?'

His softly mocking words cut like a knife. Reality crept back into her numbed brain, and she writhed in protest as she felt her nipples tug in response, felt the stirring hardness of his body against the tender ache in her groin.

'Let me go, Luc,' she whispered huskily, ashamed of the hot whirlpool of longing he'd aroused so easily inside her, and frightened, more frightened than she'd ever been, of the strength and illogical potency of her feelings for him.

Out of the corner of her eye, she caught a movement along the beach, and they both turned to see Elliot, standing on the far end of the hotel terrace, hands on hips, watching them silently.

As she struggled to free herself, deeply embarrassed, Luc tightened his hold on her, and with a triumphant gleam in his eyes bent his head to cover her protesting mouth with his, thrusting his tongue deeply inside to fence with hers until the blackness engulfed her brain again, and she found herself mindlessly responding.

When he finally released her, Elliot had disappeared. Scarlet-faced, Verity pushed at Luc's shoulders, rage surging inside her at Luc's arrogant manipulation of the situation.

'Lover-boy seems to have thrown in the towel,' Luc commented with a cruel grin, glancing at the empty spot where Elliot had stood. 'Come on, let's get you back to the villa. Your ankle's swelling again.'

'Leave me alone, Luc!' she spat in a low, furious voice, pushing away from him and gritting her teeth to limp resolutely up the beach without his help. 'When I want your help, I'll ask for it!'

'I thought you just had,' he mocked huskily, following her. 'A brave show of indifference, Verity. I eagerly await a demonstration of sexual awareness! By the way, I came to ask you to be my guest tonight. My sister and her husband are stopping over on their way from New York to Jamaica. I'd like you to meet them...'

'And if I choose to eat alone in my villa?' she queried tartly, a twinge from her ankle adding a sharper edge to her voice. 'What will be my punishment, I wonder?'

'Please,' Luc said abruptly, the mockery dying from his eyes. 'Just come. Carli and Raoul are nice people. I think you will like them.'

She swallowed, disconcerted by the silent plea in his eyes. Her imagination, she decided cynically. Luc didn't plead with anyone.

'OK,' she heard herself agreeing coolly. 'What time?'

'Nine. I will come to the villa for you.'

'No need, thanks! I *can* walk perfectly well by myself!'

Verity forced her foot to function as normally as pain would allow as she retreated towards the villa. She was conscious of Luc's eyes every step of the way. By the time she gained the privacy of her sitting-room, she felt entitled to a round of applause.

Full marks for stoical independence, she mocked herself, collapsing into a chair to massage her ankle, and staring unseeingly at the green floral curtains billowing in the breeze. And for suppressing her antagonism and agreeing to meet Luc's sister and her husband tonight, she deserved the martyr's medal, at the very least...

But, as it turned out, no medal was required. The evening turned out to be a surprising success, and Luc's older sister and her husband were so charming that it was impossible not to relax in their company.

'So you're the Verity that Luc talks about!' Carli declared, sweeping an approving gaze over Verity's simple, sleeveless white blouse and nutmeg print skirt. 'I'm so glad to meet you at last!'

Verity found herself warmly embraced on both cheeks, and drawn into the laughing group on Luc's private veranda at the end of the hotel. Pablito had met her in the terrace restaurant, where she'd automatically headed, and formally escorted her to Luc, informing her that dinner was to be served in Señor García's own suite of rooms.

Well, here, at least she'd be free from the embarrassing attentions of Elliot, Verity reflected with faint relief. And, while having dinner alone with Luc in his private suite would have presented a considerable threat to her equilibrium, there was safety in numbers.

A wide sun-veranda, screened by a lush vine pergola, was softly lit now by globe wall-lamps. There were steps down to a stretch of private beach, screened from the rest by woven bamboo fencing and thick clumps of coconut palms. A cane table and comfortable cane chairs were arranged on the veranda, and Verity was persuaded to sit down to rest her ankle, even though after a day lazing on a sun-lounger it was hardly hurting now.

But she sat down next to Carli, and found she was enjoying herself. The evening breeze rustled the palm fronds. The scent of the ocean mingled with the heady perfume of flowers, and the aroma of something deliciously spicy being prepared in the kitchen.

Raoul turned out to be a marine biologist, short and balding, with laughing brown eyes. Verity sipped the Ron Sour she'd been given, and chatted to Carli while she surreptitiously watched and listened as Raoul and Luc leaned against the veranda railings and conducted an animated discussion about the marine life off the island's coast. They'd all switched from Spanish to English as soon as she arrived, and she realised that she was seeing a new Luc, relaxed and laughing, the sardonic gleam and the cynical edge dormant for once.

In a loose, dusky blue T-shirt, the short sleeves revealing the lean muscularity of his arms, and close-fitting cream trousers which hugged the hard, athletic contours of his hips and thighs, he was overpoweringly attractive. Verity dragged her eyes away from him with an effort, her stomach twisting in knots.

Carli was telling her that she taught geography at an international school in New York, where she and Raoul lived.

'The trouble is, I love my subject, but the job is so stressful! I wish I could do what you do!' she added, tossing back her straight dark bob with a laugh. 'But

I'm the worst cook in the Western world! So I admire you even more than Luc!'

Her eyes were blue like Luc's, with an engaging frankness, their colour intensified by the rich turquoise of her silk shift-dress. It was on the tip of Verity's tongue to state that Luc did not admire her, and wasn't ever likely to, but Luc appeared beside them at that point, drawing up a chair and fixing a smiling gaze on his sister.

'I heard my name mentioned. What are you two saying about me?' he queried on a wry note.

'Carli was saying that she admires me even more than you do,' Verity echoed, meeting Luc's eyes with an ironic gleam in her own. 'She clearly hasn't appreciated how familiarity breeds contempt!'

The words were spoken jokingly, with a wide smile, but a slight chill pervaded the atmosphere between them nevertheless, and Carli glanced quickly from one to the other, a knowing gleam appearing in her eyes. Verity bit her lip in vexation. She hadn't wanted to spoil the warm, relaxed feel of the evening. Now she felt gauche and immature, and churlish... Why, oh, why had she said that?

'I detect an undercurrent,' Carli announced, with a triumphant grin. 'Don't let me get in the way if you two want to have a good row! I'll go and make small talk with Raoul!'

'Don't worry, Carli,' Luc said softly, his narrowed gaze telling Verity that he was far from pleased, 'Verity has an eccentric sense of humour. She knows that she has my... undying admiration...'

Her breath caught in her throat suddenly at the light in Luc's eyes. With a short laugh, she took a nervous sip of her drink and smiled apologetically at Carli.

'Sorry, it *was* just a joke. I didn't mean to make you feel uncomfortable!' she said, sincerity warming her voice. She liked Carli. She was one of those people she felt she'd known for years even though they'd only met ten minutes before.

'Luc told me what happened to your fiancé last year,' Carli said quietly later, while they were eating dinner around a candle-lit oval table. 'I don't wish to embarrass you. Just to say I am so very sorry, Verity...'

'Thanks. It's all right. I'm fine now...really...'

'Luc was there when it happened, *si*?'

'Yes...he...I...we both were...' Verity took a gulp of wine, and sensed that Luc had lost concentration on what Raoul was saying to him.

'And since then you've kept in touch. That must help.'

Verity stared at Carli blankly.

'To have someone to talk to, someone who knows exactly what you went through?' Carli explained, her gaze quizzical on Verity's dazed expression.

'I...yes, of course...'

Carli saw her discomfort and pulled a self-deprecating face.

'Sorry, I'm too outspoken! You still find it hard to talk about; you must have loved your fiancé very much. Forgive me, Verity——'

'Tell me about living in New York, Carli,' Verity cut in quickly, desperately switching the topic, conscious of the relentless glitter of Luc's appraisal across the table. 'Is it as lonely as people say? Do you get homesick? Are you the only García to live there, or do you have relatives near by?'

Carli smiled and raised her eyebrows at Raoul. 'New York is such an ethnic mix, we don't feel specially homesick, do we, *cara*?'

Raoul shook his head. 'For instance, Carli has ancestors from this island,' he pointed out, 'and many

Dominicans live in New York. They have transported their whole culture with them, *merengue* music, everything. And in any case, Carli is no longer a García,' he added lightly, smiling at Luc. 'As my wife, she is a de Santana.'

Verity smiled back politely, her brain racing. De Santana? Surely, a coincidence? Surely, after the way Luc had treated his wife, he couldn't be on such friendly terms with a close relative of Juliette de Santana? Luc was watching her confusion. Finally he came to her rescue.

'Raoul is a cousin of my ex-wife,' he told her flatly, with a cynical lift of his eyebrow at her shocked reaction. 'Juliette's father is Raoul's uncle.'

Dumbfounded, Verity pushed her knife and fork together, and leaned back in her chair. Her plate was still half full. The food was excellent, a mouthwatering casserole of chicken with tropical fruits and spices which Carli had called *Sancocho de Pollo*, but her tastebuds suddenly felt dry.

Carli touched her hand lightly, her eyes wryly humorous.

'Are you wondering how Luc can bear to fraternise with another de Santana?' she murmured, surprisingly. 'Well, first of all, I am Luc's only sister, and Luc loves me, and since I am married to Raoul, and nothing is going to change that, we are all, still, very good friends!'

'I'm afraid I don't quite understand...' Verity heard herself saying slowly, abruptly thrown into complete bewilderment, her eyes caught and held by the hard, wary expression on Luc's face.

'Verity is not interested in our family dramas, Carli,' he snapped warningly, but his elder sister blithely ignored him.

'Blood may be thicker than water, Verity,' Carli was continuing firmly, 'but, while Juliette's present plight is enough to arouse anyone's sympathy, it is only Federico de Santana, Juliette's father, who remains blinkered and loyal enough to idolise his daughter after her appalling behaviour during her marriage to Luc!'

CHAPTER SIX

'I'M SORRY,' Verity said with stiff formality, finally breaking the heavy silence as Luc walked her back along the beach towards her villa. 'It seems as if I've listened to some ill-founded rumours and judged you... rather unfairly...'

'Is that so?' Luc's voice was ominously soft. She should have registered that warning tone by now, associated it with danger signals. But she was too preoccupied with her own outraged sense of truthfulness. She knew how it felt to be unfairly accused on moral issues, didn't she? Luc's scathing indictment of her fidelity after that episode between them last year had cut like a knife. But even so, if she'd allowed malicious scandal-mongering to cloud her opinion of Luc's character last year, then she felt honour-bound to right the wrong, as fast as possible, whatever the personal embarrassment...

'I hate gossip,' she went on doggedly, 'but at the time I saw no reason to disbelieve it.'

'Indeed? And why was that, I wonder? Because I looked like the kind of man who would willingly throw his wife on the scrap-heap because she had developed a fault?'

'No, I...' She was floundering, put on the defensive again. Luc was impossible. But so was this situation. Why *had* she instantly believed that story about his wife? It had been the wife of one of the other polo players who'd relayed the information. Completely false information, if tonight was anything to go by. Had she been eager to believe the worst because it relieved her guilt about Edward?

'So now you're prepared to reconsider your opinion of me? How magnanimous!'

There was no mistaking the cool cynicism this time.

'Luc, please...'

'Since you're so addicted to gossip, would you like the whole sordid little tale, Verity?'

They'd stopped outside the shadowy garden of the villa, and she stared at him. His face was taut and harsh in the moonlight.

'Luc... you're not making it very easy for me to apologise——' she began in a hoarse voice, but he cut across her abruptly.

'Then don't apologise,' he suggested shortly. 'There was no reason for you to trust me, any more than there was for me to trust you! Maybe neither of us is the trusting type!'

She swallowed, digging her nails into her palms to control her temper. Her ankle was aching, and she shifted her weight, surreptitiously massaging it against the back of her other leg.

It was harder to trust people who had the power to hurt you... easier when getting hurt or disillusioned or deserted wasn't such a risk... The thought crept into her head, and she caught her breath abruptly, alarmed by the implication.

'What did happen, Luc? With your wife?'

Her shaky query brought a harsh laugh in the darkness.

'So you do want the sordid details, Verity? I thought you might!'

'Luc, that's not fair!'

'No... maybe not.' He sounded as though the anger had abruptly faded. With a brief, slightly unsteady hand he reached to touch her cheek, then he turned away. 'Sorry, I'm in no mood to discuss the vicissitudes of my disastrous marriage tonight. Go to bed, Verity. I'll see you tomorrow.'

She hesitated, glancing at his intractable profile. 'I liked your sister and her husband...'

The look he turned on her was wryly mocking. 'So you'll come out for the day with us tomorrow?'

'Yes.'

'*Bueno. Que duermas bien.*'

'Goodnight, Luc.'

She was conscious of his eyes following her as she made her way slowly towards the villa garden and the glowing lights of the terrace. But he made no move to come after her. To her eternal chagrin she realised that she wanted him to. She wanted him to trust her enough to confide in her... she wanted... she wanted... no, she wasn't sure what she wanted.

When she reached the villa she looked round, but he'd already disappeared. The sense of angry frustration stayed with her, keeping her awake long after she'd showered and lain down on her bed to sleep.

She dreamed about a polo match, full of the distorted thunder of hoofbeats, the dust and excitement and tension. Then the familiar images jumbled, blurred into a sensual excitement burning between herself and the warm male body holding her close, moving rhythmically, dancing on a strangely surreal polo field, alone, and yet surrounded by the swirling polo match in progress and the spectators who'd come to watch.

It was Edward's arms, she was almost certain, Edward whose arms she was dancing in, whose closeness was igniting this fire of desire inside her. And then the horseman was thundering towards them, his face shadowed beneath his helmet and protective visor, stick raised high above his head, riding straight at them, and they dived for the ground, dived for cover and the rider swerved to avoid them, and crashed off the horse, hitting the ground with an audible thud to lie very still, too still...

Verity was sobbing, clutching him in her arms, but when she saw his face...it was Luc, not Edward...and she was screaming, screaming Luc's name and falling, falling...

With a start she found herself bolt upright in bed, in a tangle of sweat-soaked sheets. Trembling, she stared wildly into the darkness, then reached for the bedside lamp, clicked it on, and sank back shakily on to her pillows. She hadn't had the nightmare for months. Exhausted, she shrank from turning off the light again. The images stayed in her head too long. It was always a struggle to clear her mind of the stubborn wisps of the nightmare, and they seemed more disturbing in the darkness.

Why did the early hours magnify everything, make every problem loom ten times more intolerable? It was at times like these that she grieved most keenly for her mother. She'd loved her father too, and she missed him terribly despite everything...

But she missed her mother in some deep, primeval way she couldn't explain. It wasn't as if they'd been all that close. Father's army career had meant world-wide travel for her parents, and long stays in boarding-school for Verity. Those remembered nature walks together had been a rarity, rather than the norm. Perhaps that was why they'd stayed so vividly in her mind.

But that almost made it worse. She'd never had a chance to really get to *know* her mother... to cross that child-parent relationship and achieve the enviable closeness she watched other girls of her age enjoying, out shopping, or having coffee with their mothers, chatting, confiding, sharing their greatest triumphs, finding comfort when things went wrong...

Sometimes, when she thought about it, she felt bitterly angry, betrayed, deserted. Which was confusing. How could she feel *angry* with her parents for getting themselves killed?

After tossing and turning, she finally got up and went to get a drink of lime juice from the fridge, wandering out on to the terrace and collapsing into a low wicker sun-lounger to sip the drink thoughtfully. She found herself cursing Luc García for his misguided notion of enforced relaxation.

She was fine as long as she stayed busy, wasn't she? Abandoned to her own devices, she turned into a self-pitying wreck! Was that what this was all about? Luc's twisted idea of punishment for her perfidy over Edward? Was this fortnight to ensure that she sweated it out, relived the past, endured suitable suffering to mark the memory of Edward's death?

'You look rather pale, Verity,' Carli commented next morning, inspecting her strained pallor and dark-smudged eyes as they drove east along the coast. 'Are you feeling unwell?'

'I had a restless night,' Verity confessed, watching the passing scenery from the open jeep. After the endless introspection of the night, she'd felt desperate to avoid coming on this outing, but, short of offending Carli, no solution had presented itself. Her nerves felt shredded at the prospect of a day constantly in Luc's company, of a drive sitting a mere foot away from him, separated only by the width of a gear-stick. She felt tense, and churned up inside, aware of Luc to such a degree that every tiny hair on her body stood erect in its follicle, the primitive signal for fight or flight...

The weather seemed to mirror her mood as they followed the coastal road through pastures and sugar cane and coconut palm plantations, where rows of nuts lay germinating on the ground, sprouting green shoots. The sun was beating down, hot on her shoulders, so that she was glad of the short sleeves of her cream cotton top to protect her skin, and the vivid blue of the Atlantic was never far from view, but there were black clouds banking on the horizon. A tropical storm appeared to be brewing out to the north-east. A brooding sense of imminent eruption hung in the air.

'I think we're in for some rain.' Luc glanced across at her with a cool half-grin, his gaze briefly catching Verity's before he returned his eyes to the road. He seemed harder, more disturbingly attractive than ever, clad in rough, stone-washed denim shirt, open-necked, sleeves pushed up over powerful forearms, and close-fitting denim jeans. Dragging her eyes away from the strong, muscular arm changing gear, and the dark-tanned nape of his neck where the thick black hair tapered to a neat point, she smoothed shaky fingers over her bare knees. Her hands felt restless. She found herself fidgeting uncharacteristically, pleating the sage-green fabric of her shorts before sitting resolutely on her hands to control her nerves.

'No problem. I can cope with a spot of warm rain,' she said lightly, searching for her sunglasses and slotting them on. She felt she needed to hide behind something. Luc seemed more abrasive, the electric gaze more intent than normal today. 'Sara said on the phone yesterday that it was actually trying to *snow* in London!' she added, forcing a laugh over her shoulder at Carli and Raoul. 'Can you believe that? In mid-April?'

'Give me a tropical rainstorm any day!' Raoul laughed.

It was an action-packed day. Carli wanted to revisit as many favourite spots as possible before leaving for Jamaica in the morning. They drove to Cabarete Beach, and watched the windsurfers doing impossible manoeuvres on the rolling waves, then on along the coast to Gri-Gri Lagoon, and took a boat ride up between the strange, stilt-like grey roots of the mangroves. The rain stubbornly refused to come, and the air grew heavier, more clouds banking on the far horizon. Verity felt no let-up in the edgy mood which gripped her.

After a mouthwatering lunch of shellfish and salads back in Sosua, they split up for half an hour while Luc sought out a horse-dealer friend and Verity followed Carli and Raoul on a leisurely browse around the boutiques and souvenir shops. Lost in preoccupation, and dazed after her sleepless night, Verity took a while to realise that she'd lost sight of the others. Wandering from shop to shop, buying every unusual tropical fruit and vegetable she could find, to experiment with back at the villa tonight, she'd somehow ended up in a narrower, poorer side-street, and she stopped, unsure of her bearings for a few seconds.

She was quickly reassured. At the far end of the dusty little street she could see the market square and the 'lorry-bank', where they'd exchanged US dollars for Dominican pesos a little earlier, guarded by the armed soldiers who frequently roamed the island. She wasn't far from civilisation.

A stall selling fresh pineapples caught her eye, and she stopped, clutching her bag of vegetables, haltingly asking the price in her scanty Spanish.

'*Un peso*,' the boy grinned, tossing a whole fruit from one hand to another and proceeding to wield a vicious-looking machete with heart-stopping accuracy. Within seconds the fruit was sliced and presented to her on clean paper, with a flourish.

'*Gracias*!' Verity beamed, delighted. She offered the boy two pesos, unthinkingly, and then suspected that she'd made a mistake when she attracted attention from a group of women near by. She'd forgotten that the Dominican Republic was virtually a Third World country. You were expected to haggle over prices, not throw your money around as if it meant nothing...

A smiling, plump woman of around thirty strolled to join them, eyeing Verity up and down with undisguised interest.

'*Americana*? *Inglesa*?'

'English,' Verity affirmed, smiling back rather uncertainly. The woman wore a yellow woven scarf covering her hair, a long black dress and large golden earrings. She had a gypsy look about her. Unexpectedly blue eyes studied Verity's sun-flushed skin exposed by the thin cotton top and shorts.

'English?' The woman echoed, nodding. 'For *dos pesos*, I read *su mano*...?'

Verity frowned. The sun was hot, and the pineapple juice was beginning to run down between her fingers. *Su mano*—her hand. The woman wanted to read her palm?

The boy behind the stall grinned at her, shrugging apologetically.

'*Mi hermana*—my sister?' he told her, demonstrating a surprising grasp of English. '*Se llama Rosalina*. Her name is Rosalina. She read your palm...' His accent was strong, but Verity was impressed nevertheless. 'Tell your future, *si*?'

'*Si, si*.' The woman was nodding furiously, grasping Verity's right hand and studying the radiating lines with a deep frown of concentration. Too surprised to argue, Verity put her pineapple down on the front of the fruit-stall with her other hand, and licked her sticky fingers and shrugged and laughed.

'OK, why not? What do you see?'

After a long spate of rapid Spanish, as Rosalina ran her finger along each of the linear channels in Verity's palm, the Spanish woman abruptly dropped her hand and clapped in smiling triumph.

'*Bueno*! *Bueno*!' she exclaimed in obvious delight, surprising Verity even more by grasping her shoulders and kissing her enthusiastically on each cheek. '*Suerte*! *Que tengas suerte, señorita*!'

'*Suerte*? Luck?' Verity translated, proud of herself as Rosalina laughed and nodded. 'Good luck, I hope, not bad!'

'*Si, si*, good luck! *Vas a casarte con un hombre muy guapo, pronto, pronto*!'

Verity raised an eyebrow at the fruit-seller for translation, who grinned even wider.

'You will marry a very...*beautiful* man! Very soon!' he informed her, as Verity's eyes widened in amazement, and she burst out laughing, shaking her head.

'Oh, I don't think so!'

'*Si, es verdad*!' Rosalina smiled, picking up Verity's denial and touching her lightly on the cheek. '*Vamos a ver*! Let us see!'

'How soon?' Verity challenged good-humouredly, fumbling for two more pesos in her purse and willingly handing them over. '*Cuándo*? When? When will the wedding be?'

'*Este año*!' Rosalina affirmed positively, her eyes dancing at Verity's disbelief. 'This year!'

'And what will my husband look like?' Verity wanted to know, wryly playing along with the joke, grappling with her sixth-form Spanish for the right words. 'Tall—er—dark?'

'*Si*!' Rosalina agreed, rather too readily to be remotely convincing, Verity thought privately. '*Alto y moreno*! Tall and dark!'

'Well, thank you!' Verity laughed, retrieving her pineapple, and her shopping bag. '*Muchas gracias, señora*!'

Thank you very much for the biggest load of make-believe since Peter Pan, Verity reflected, as she made her way back towards the square to find Luc's jeep, eating the lusciously sweet and juicy pineapple as she walked. She felt more relaxed. The incident had somehow imparted a touch of enjoyable local colour to her day.

They were all waiting for her at the jeep when she arrived. Suddenly sheepish, Verity was conscious of her disreputable appearance, covered in sticky pineapple juice, sucking the fruit from the last knobbly wedge of skin. Half laughing, half embarrassed, she apologised for holding everyone up while she dug in her shoulder-bag for a tissue, avoiding Luc's piercingly intent gaze as he watched every move she made.

Carli had bought jewellery, a long-sleeved shirt, and two leather belts, and had been exhibiting her finds to Luc as Verity returned.

The hoard of exotic foods in Verity's possession provoked a teasing reaction.

'Trust Verity to buy food,' Luc commented drily, the blue gaze wryly amused as she scrubbed at the sticky juice on her mouth. 'She's already devising half a dozen new uses for pineapple to add to her menus.'

'Then Verity's business will thrive!' Raoul declared approvingly as they all climbed into the jeep. 'Such single-minded concentration!'

When she briefly mentioned her palm-reading, Carli clapped her hands in delight.

'You've met one of the island's "witches",' she laughed. 'There are lots of them. They read coffee-cups, or tarot cards, or candle flames, all sorts of strange methods! Did she predict your future, *cara*?'

'Yes, but not terribly convincingly!' Verity grinned. 'She predicted a wedding, by the end of the year!'

Carli's dark eyebrows rose.

'For you?'

'Yes!'

'So?' she teased. 'Is that so impossible? It is now only the middle of April! A lot can happen in nine months!'

'Well, since I've no intention of *ever* marrying,' Verity pointed out succinctly, 'I'd need a major brainstorm coupled with convenient amnesia before my witch's wedding took place!'

Carli said nothing, the expression in her eyes suggesting that out of deference to Verity's past tragedy she felt it wiser to drop the subject.

'I thought convenient amnesia was already a well-practised art of yours,' Luc purred silkily, as Verity

turned back to the front. 'We'll call at Casa Cordera on
our way back. I want to take a look at this season's new
foals...'

She forced herself to maintain a dignified silence. Luc's
gibe had been too soft to be heard by the passengers in
the rear but, even so, she wasn't going to be goaded into
a slanging match in the company of others, if she could
possibly help it...

The Casa Cordera turned out to be a colonial-style
farmhouse, which combined horse-breeding with fruit,
coffee and coconut plantations, complete with resident
housekeeper, butler, maids and ranch-hands.

Verity sat with Carli on the long, raised, pillared stone
terrace which flanked all four sides of the building,
sipping a glass of iced papaya punch under the shade of
a massive royal palm, and gazing in disbelief at her surroundings. A shady, stone-walled garden gave way to
rolling pastureland. As she watched, a cluster of magnificent horses cantered into view and then split up and
galloped off in different directions, manes and tails
flying. They were a long way off, but their hoofbeats
were just discernible in the warm, heavy silence of the
afternoon.

'I knew Luc had a ranch here,' she told Carli, as the
other woman rocked to and fro lazily in a swing-chair.
The two men had disappeared into the stables, leaving
them to cool down and relax out of the increasingly
stormy heat. 'But I didn't expect anything quite like this!
I assumed that the hotel in Puerto Plata would be his
main property...'

'My brother is a man of hidden assets,' Carli agreed
drily. 'I always think that was why Juliette was so determined to hang on to him. She was determined to

remain living "in the style to which she'd become accustomed", as I think you say, even after everything that happened.'

'What *did* happen?' Verity blurted out, without meaning to. Carli shot her a thoughtful look, and Verity felt her cheeks grow pinker.

'Luc hasn't told you?'

'No...'

'Do you care about my brother, Verity?' Carli's voice held a gently curious note, but there was warmth in her blue eyes as she watched for a reaction.

Verity felt a gripping, tightening sensation somewhere in the region of her solar plexus. Her throat drying, she evaded the other girl's eyes.

'Not...not in the sense that I think you mean,' she hedged, scarlet now beneath the frankly disbelieving gaze of Luc's sister. 'I'm not sure how I'd describe our relationship...'

Pushing a hand through her shiny black cap of hair, Carli smiled.

'I'm no fool, Verity. There is an electric atmosphere between you two. Last night, and again today... But I don't want to pry.'

'You're wrong.' Verity's heart was thudding idiotically as she shrank from confronting her own emotions. 'There's nothing like that at all...'

Carli was silent for a long moment. Finally, she said thoughtfully, 'Luc finds it really hard to talk about Juliette. But I think you should know some of it, even though he'll strangle me when he finds out I told you. They met at my wedding to Raoul. Juliette was only seventeen, incredibly beautiful, incredibly wilful. Her mother died when she was ten, and she'd been pampered and indulged by her father ever since. Luc was only twenty-three, and to be quite honest he was rather... headstrong! He took one look at Juliette and he was infatuated with her. Only when they'd married, it turned out she'd been pregnant already, by a lover who'd abandoned her. Luc came along just in time to save her reputation...'

'How did Luc find out?'

'The ex-lover reappeared. He actually demanded blood tests for paternity, and proved the child was his!'

'Oh! How awful.' Verity breathed shakily, her imagination speared by the image of Luc's shattered pride.

Carli was watching her appalled reaction with calm interest.

'There was an enormous row. But neither family approved of divorce, of course,' she went on quietly, 'and Juliette swore blind she loved Luc, she wanted to stay with him, begged him to forgive her. Mind you, the baby's real father was very poor. I suspect that's one reason why she made a bee-line for Luc in the first place. Anyway, Luc *did* make a valiant effort to forgive her. We all thought he was crazy. I mean, it wasn't so much her initial mistake—we are all human, after all. Anyone can make a mistake. But it was the... cold-blooded deception. She deliberately made a fool of Luc. But my brother has very... noble... *old-fashioned* views about the sanctity of marriage.'

Verity had to suppress a groan of anguish. Her self-righteous, disapproving comments to Luc about his marriage seemed to echo in her head. She felt a wave of shame at her readiness to brand him an immoral cheat.

'But I think he was so hurt and disillusioned, he couldn't forget it,' Carli was continuing thoughtfully. 'They kept going as a family unit for a few months, but grew further and further apart. I think he felt that he could never trust her again. She'd lied to him, made a fool of him, and he couldn't forgive her. Finally, she had an affair with a fellow polo player, right under Luc's nose. Luc started divorce proceedings...'

'And then Juliette became ill?'

'A few months after the divorce came through. She'd gone back to live with the ex-lover, the father of her son. Supported, I might add, by *her* father, Federico——'

'What happened to the baby?' Verity cut in, appalled.

'The ex-lover took him. I think he married someone else. Juliette still gets visits from him, but I gather she's not terribly bothered about keeping in touch with her son. Unbelievable, isn't it? But, to be fair, the poor girl has paid for her sins!' Carli said wryly. 'She hasn't walked for years. She's in a private, luxurious nursing home in Florida, where they have access to every conceivable new treatment and drug and medical opinion. Luc pays an annual contribution towards it all. I'm not really sure why—her father has a chain of hotels in America and he's rich as Croesus. I suspect, to a degree, it's this misguided sense of honour Luc has. Even after what happened between them, Juliette was once his wife, and he feels somehow...responsible for her welfare.'

Carli's confidences haunted Verity for the rest of their stay at the ranch, long after Luc and Raoul returned from the paddocks to persuade them to come for a ride.

Sitting rather nervously astride a docile bay gelding, she turned the information over and over in her mind as she watched Luc's impressive expertise on a powerful chestnut stallion.

Edward's words came back to her, as she watched him. Natural riders like Luc had an in-built advantage on the polo field, she remembered Edward saying enviously. They didn't even need to think about riding a horse.

They didn't need to think about whether the horse would turn or not, when they went after the ball... they sat and rode so effortlessly that it helped them to move faster in the field.

Why had Edward never told her about Luc's disastrous marriage? Had he merely been respecting Luc's confidence? Luc had said something which mystified her recently...something about Edward being a loyal friend, helping him over a difficult time in his life. He must have been referring to Juliette. Edward must have known all about it, despite being three years younger; he must have been Luc's chief confidant...certainly, Edward had known Luc long enough...

She was lost in thought, as they all drove back to Puerto Plata. Luc talked over his shoulder to Carli and Raoul, glancing at her from time to time, noting her preoccupation without comment.

Back at the hotel, she pleaded a headache and excused herself from eating a farewell meal with them all. She needed time alone, to think her way carefully through her feelings. She had an overwhelming longing to really *talk* to Luc, to examine whatever tenuous relationship they might have, to air the hidden undercurrents which seemed to continually block communication.

'I've enjoyed meeting you,' she amended hastily, seeing Carli's obvious disappointment. 'Perhaps I'll see you before you go tomorrow?'

'That would be nice.' Carli kissed her cheek, and searched her eyes briefly before smiling and turning to follow Raoul back into the hotel.

Verity glanced at Luc's inscrutable expression, and hesitated just a fraction too long before swinging away towards the villa. He followed her and caught her arm, his gaze oddly dissecting as he scanned her face.

'Why won't you join us for a meal tonight?'

'I . . . I need some time on my own . . .'

The brilliant blue eyes narrowed thoughtfully on her stubborn expression. Then he shrugged and released her arm, running his hand over the beginnings of five o'clock stubble on his chin.

'Is it your ankle? Have you overdone it today?'

'No, my ankle's fine.'

'But you're allergic to my company.'

'No!'

She tensed at the darkening of his gaze as he stared at her. There was an awkward pause as she fought the whirl of unexplained emotions circling inside her.

'No, Verity?' They were standing among the hibiscus trees at the side of the pool, near the path to the villa, with guests and staff passing frequently either side of them, but for a breathless few seconds she felt as if only she and Luc existed, the magnetic pull between them felt so overpowering.

'I'm . . . I'm sorry I was so rude about your marriage . . . I'm sorry if I misjudged you . . . about Juliette,' she said in a sudden, impulsive rush, her voice low and intense. 'Last night, you wouldn't let me apologise, and you wouldn't explain . . .'

A shuttered look had crept back into Luc's eyes.

'And today you imagine things are different?' he drawled laconically. 'I gather Carli's been expounding on the subject?'

'We did talk, yes.'

His mouth twisted in a cold travesty of a smile, and her heart contracted abruptly at the chilling intensity of his eyes.

'My marriage to Juliette was an unfortunate error,' he said shortly. 'It's over, finished, history. It's not a subject I care to discuss.'

'How can you say that?' she shot back softly, dimly aware that she was feeling angry and frustrated by his refusal to confide in her, and incredulous that she should feel like this. 'How can you claim it's over, finished, when you're still so *involved* with her?'

'What are you talking about?' The tightness of his voice warned her of the extent of his controlled anger.

'I'm talking about how you're paying towards her nursing home fees, as if *you* have some . . . some guilt to expiate! From what Carli said, you're the last person who needs to feel guilty!'

There was a long, charged silence. Verity thrust a trembling hand through her hair, and gazed in wide-eyed anguish at Luc's deadpan expression. With him standing there motionless in front of her, in the rough denim shirt and jeans, the dark hair falling in the familiar unruly lock over his forehead, she had the strangest sensation that a chasm was opening up between them, even wider than before. Instead of feeling closer to him, instead of sensing a glimmer of understanding between them, he suddenly looked darker, more distant, more aggressively foreign and masculine and alarming.

'What a tragedy I didn't consult you months ago,' he retorted at last, softly mocking, 'Then all my problems could have been solved in one easy stroke.'

Her cheeks were burning. The depth of bitterness in his eyes was frightening.

'Luc, you're not being very fair . . .'

'I should have remembered that you're an authority on the psychology of guilt, Verity,' he added ruthlessly. 'Maybe we should get together and compare notes!'

A coldness had crept into her. With a sharp breath, she caught herself up impatiently, slamming her emotions into reverse. This was impossible. What an idiot she was, to imagine that Carli's brief insight into Luc's past had given her any firmer basis for understanding him. What was she thinking of, trying to get closer to him? That was the *last* thing she wanted, wasn't it?

'We'll talk later,' he added on a harsh note of dismissal. 'There are some things I need to attend to now.'

He was turning on his heel and striding away before she had time to argue.

Seething inwardly, she made her way back to the villa, where the humid heat of the day seemed slightly less oppressive in the cooling trade winds off the sea.

What did he mean by 'later'? she wondered furiously. She fully intended an early night. So Luc could forget about seeing her 'later'. The way she felt tonight, she'd be happy if she never had to see him again.

A shower and hair-wash went some way to restoring her shaken spirits, and after smoothing on musk-scented moisturiser and talcum powder she felt even calmer. Slipping into an ivory silk crop-top and matching calf-length skirt, and tying her damp hair up in a loose topknot, she padded barefoot around the silent villa, debating whether to ring for a quick supper to be sent over from the hotel, then decided that cooking would be therapeutic.

Her head hurt with the maelstrom of conflicting ideas circling in her mind. She needed solitude. The fridge was well stocked, and cooking was no chore—it was one of her favourite occupations. It was something she was lucky enough to be able to do with such practised ease that she could do it when she wanted to empty her mind, shelve her problems and just let her thoughts drift mindlessly. She'd cook for herself, experimenting with her new purchases, then eat in solitary splendour, reading the historical romance novel she'd started on the plane. She felt badly in need of some routine relaxation tonight, time alone to switch off and recharge her batteries.

Knotting a tea-towel round her waist as a makeshift apron, within an hour she'd assembled a delicately exotic supper, and with a tray in her hands she went out to the terrace to lay the table.

The abrupt tropical darkness had already fallen. With the storm clouds still heavy in the air, the night seemed even darker than usual. Even the moonlight was missing. The wind was rustling the palm trees, and the night sounds seemed louder than normal, the cicadas' monotonous shrilling almost deafening.

She reached for the switch to illuminate the terrace lights, just as the figure which detached itself from the shadows in the corner appeared so unexpectedly that she almost dropped the tray.

'Evening, Verity...' Elliot moved into the light from one of the storm-lanterns on the villa's wall, and Verity sighed in exasperation. She hadn't seen him since he'd called at the villa yesterday, and, after a brief conversation which spelt out her feelings in no uncertain terms, she'd secretly hoped he might have packed up and gone.

'Hello, Elliot.'

'Don't look like that,' he complained, his voice plaintive yet oddly apologetic. 'Just called by to say I'm leaving tomorrow. Thought I'd tour round a bit—explore some more of the island...'

A flood of relief made her smile at him with more warmth, but then, as he lurched towards her, she sighed. He was holding a half-empty bottle of red wine in one hand, and a glass in the other.

'Got the message,' he added, his voice rather slurred, 'when I saw you in that clinch on the beach yesterday morning.'

'I'm sorry you flew all the way out here, thinking...' She stopped uncertainly, deciding the least said, the better on whatever Elliot might have thought.

'Ah, well, that's life...' He put the bottle and the glass down clumsily on the patio table, narrowly missing the tray she'd placed there, and fixed her with an unfocused gaze. 'Going to join me in a farewell drink, sweetheart?'

'No, thanks. You look as if you've drunk enough already, Elliot!'

'Well, what's a chap supposed to do when he flies all this way to see the lady he loves and all he gets is...*ignored*?' he began sorrowfully. 'How was I supposed to know you had the hots for some womanising South American polo player who thinks he's God's gift to women?'

'I haven't got the "hots" for anyone,' she retorted indignantly, 'and you're lucky you haven't got sunstroke, looking at the colour of your skin!'

Against his red sports shirt, and white shorts, the skin on his legs and arms looked raw. The habitual golden tan he sported on his face was probably out of a bottle, Verity reflected, with a twinge of sympathy.

'I'm perfectly all right...' Elliot got his tongue around the words with a degree of difficulty '...and I'll be even better when I finish this bottle of wine.'

'Come on, no more. You're already drunk. You'd better get back to your hotel room and sleep it off!' she suggested calmly, moving to try to steer him off the terrace. It was a mistake. Leaning against her drunkenly, he swayed heavily and knocked her off balance, bumping her into the table, which rocked precariously with its

load of food and wine. As she braced herself to take his
weight he trod on her bare toe. Verity let out a yelp of
pain, her injured ankle gave way, and together they
toppled over, sending the table and its contents hurtling
to the floor with a resounding crash.

In the ensuing chaos, Verity heard a shout of other
voices in the darkness beyond the palms. And then she
recognised Luc's furious voice, harshly controlled,
rapping out curt orders in Spanish as he strode up to
witness the unsavoury scenario on the villa's terrace.
Bruised and dishevelled, she struggled to her feet, to see
Luc grab Elliot with laconic ease, pinning the English-
man's arms behind his back as he hauled him upright.

'I want you out of here,' he growled, his voice soft
with suppressed fury. 'Now!'

'Get your hands off me...' Elliot began belligerently,
struggling to free himself, but Luc was coldly imper-
vious. With an icily controlled gesture he beckoned
Pablito and another of the hotel's strapping young
waiters, who were hovering obediently on the sidelines,
and with a dismissive thrust he transferred Elliot to their
custody, and turned away.

Verity watched, appalled, as they began to frog-march
a loudly protesting Elliot away.

White-faced, she put one hand to steady herself on
the wooden railing surrounding the terrace, trying to
collect her scattered wits.

The floor of the terrace was littered with broken glass
and crockery, and the remains of her untasted supper.
Her cream silk outfit was stained with red wine. She had
bumps and bruises in half a dozen places. And Luc's
expression, when she finally trusted herself to lift her
eyes to his, held a chilling fury which made her stomach
contract into painful knots.

'Just what the hell was going on here?'

'I'm sorry about the broken plates and glasses,' she began with quiet anger. 'I'll pay for them, of course...'

'I asked what was going on, Verity?'

'Nothing was "going on",' she shot back. 'Not that it's any of your business! Elliot was drunk,' she added, as calmly as she could. 'All he needs is time to sleep it off.'

'Not on my property.'

'What's that supposed to mean?'

'Your friend Grosvenor can find himself another hotel.'

'What? You mean your...your *henchmen* are throwing him out?' she shot back incredulously. 'You can't do that, Luc!'

She spun round to go after them, but Luc's hand shot out to detain her, his fingers digging into her arm with an effortless strength she found both infuriating and defeating.

'No?' He flexed his shoulders laconically, his expression distinctly unpleasant as he swept his gaze over the mess surrounding them, and then turned his eyes broodingly on Verity. 'I've just done it,' he drawled coldly. 'And if he returns again to make a nuisance of himself, I will not hesitate to use my influence to have him thrown off the island!'

CHAPTER SEVEN

FOR several seconds neither spoke. Verity was so angry that she didn't trust herself to speak. Outraged golden eyes fought silently with narrowed, cynical blue. Finally, drawing a long, calming breath, she lifted her arm free of Luc's fingers with exaggerated care, stepping away from his disturbing nearness. He'd swapped the denim jeans and shirt for relaxed-looking beige chinos, a loose collarless white shirt and a navy cotton waistcoat worn unbuttoned, but he still managed to exude an air of controlled menace.

'How dare you treat a friend of mine like that?' she demanded, her voice low and intense with pent-up anger. 'Elliot's only crime was to drink a drop too much wine and stumble over my foot! I could quite easily have handled the situation myself...besides, for your information, Elliot dropped by tonight to tell me he was planning on leaving tomorrow, anyway!'

'Then he will merely be leaving a little earlier.' Luc sounded coolly unrepentant. 'According to my staff, Grosvenor has been making a damn nuisance of himself all day. He's been drinking non-stop and annoying other people around the pool. As owner of this hotel I reserve the right to eject unwelcome guests.'

'Oh, I see, so the fact that Elliot appears to be in hot pursuit of me had nothing to do with this display of...of petty *despotism*?'

The blue glitter of his eyes darkened. A hint of amusement quirked at the side of his mouth.

'Why should it?' he mocked softly, stepping closer again. A clap of thunder sounded overhead, making Verity jump edgily, and massive spots of rain began pattering down on to the terrace. 'Are you suggesting that I am also in hot pursuit of you, Verity?'

The deepening of his voice sent tremors of reaction all the way down to the base of her spine, but her eyes felt riveted by his lazy gaze.

'Well?' she whispered furiously. 'Aren't you?'

What was she *saying*?

'Would you like me to be?' he murmured, silkily sardonic.

'*No*!'

As she spoke, the skies abruptly opened, the sporadic raindrops escalating into such an unexpected deluge that it was like standing under a shower. Within seconds, they were both drenched, their clothes plastered against their skin.

Luc propelled her inside, and they stood dripping on the wide honey-brown tiles of the sitting-room floor, staring at each other like fighters at the end of a round, while the tropical storm raged outside.

'No?' he mocked, a dangerous gleam in his eyes. 'Are you sure, Verity?'

The blue gaze travelled slowly downwards, from her dripping gold-brown topknot to the softly compressed curve of her lips, continued down her throat to linger with lazy appreciation on the clear outline of her breasts beneath the soaked, clinging cream silk of her crop-top. Braless beneath the wet fabric, and breathing jerkily with suppressed emotion, Verity realised with a surge of self-consciousness that she might just as well be posing topless in front of him. Colour suffused her whole body as he continued to stare, eyes narrowed, completely unabashed.

'There is something curiously erotic,' he murmured huskily, his eyes inscrutable, 'about naked breasts beneath a wet silk blouse...'

'Stop it!' she snapped, incensed, crossing her arms to cover herself. 'That just about sums you up, Luc! You see females in terms of what is sexually available, what is erotic...you're shallow, egotistical, chauvinistic...no wonder your life is one long succession of brainless bimbos since your marriage broke up.'

'Is it?' His ominously quiet voice cut across her outburst, and she stared at him in sudden horror, truly appalled at the torrent of words she'd just heard herself fling at him. He stepped close, caught hold of her hands and pulled them roughly away from her breasts, his face a dark mask of mockery. 'And what is *your* life, Verity, since Edward died? One long succession of Elliot Grosvenors? Men rich enough to pander to your whims, men weak enough to keep dangling on the promise of sexual gratification?'

White-faced, she twisted furiously in his grip as his gaze raked the outline of her body, observing the traitorous jut of her breasts, the tell-tale hardening of her nipples. Verity felt mesmerised, vulnerable, yet unsure how to protect herself. For some reason the anger she felt at Luc's arrogance was subtly commuting itself to that insane, inner longing she recognised and feared. Fury at her own weakness lent an added tartness to her voice as she bit out,

'You know *nothing* about me, nothing but the superficial conclusions you've jumped to since we met...'

'You're wrong,' he returned softly, his voice mocking. 'Edward told me all about you, Verity. He was besotted with you. I know you went to a boarding convent, that your best subjects were maths and home economics, that your shoe size is six, your taste in music ranges from Scottish folk ballads to Otis Redding. I know you like your coffee white and your favourite foods are pasta, salads, and fish; I know the style of clothes, even the style of underwear you prefer—oyster silk camisoles and French knickers—right down to your bra size, when you bother to wear one...'

'Well, if that's the way you get your kicks!' she snapped furiously, hating the taunting, mocking voice, trying to wrestle free of his grip but failing ignominiously, succeeding only in escalating the mounting tension between them as her thighs brushed against his.

'The only thing I've yet to discover,' he finished up softly, 'is your preferences in bed...'

Verity's temper erupted. Wrenching a hand free with a sudden burst of angry strength, she lashed at his face, kicking at his shins and cursing her lack of shoes. Bare feet made ineffectual weapons. Luc stood immobile under the furious onslaught, and then abruptly hauled her hard against him, flattening her against his lean height, one hand pressing the small of her back ruthlessly to seal intimate contact between their lower bodies, the other snaking into her hair to destroy the wet topknot and tangle possessively in the damp tumble of curls which cascaded around his fingers.

Pulling her head back, he bent to cover her open mouth with his own, plunging his tongue deeply and demandingly into her mouth, moving sinuously and skilfully against her as he drew her into the expert web of seduction. In the mindless few seconds which followed, while she writhed and fought the assault on her senses, Verity dimly began to realise that until now she'd experienced only a fraction of the potent sexual magnetism Luc was capable of unleashing on the unsuspecting female population.

Locked to him, with the clean, spicy scent of his skin swamping her senses, and the whip-cord strength of his limbs branding his shape against her, she finally stopped fighting him, and the kiss gradually lost some of its brutal insistence, warmed and developed a new sensitivity which seemed to release a hidden floodgate inside her, a river of liquid fire flowing into her stomach and thighs.

'Verity... *Dios*, Verity...' he groaned against her lips, lifting a slightly unsteady hand to trace the swollen outline of her mouth with one long brown finger. 'I want you... you want me too, I can feel it in the way your body moves against mine.' His eyes were heavily lidded, the pupils dilated, the brilliant blue of the irises glittering dangerously.

Heat burned through her at the expression in his eyes, the husky plea in his words. Luc García, the great womaniser, *pleading* with her? She shuddered against him, and he tightened his hold again. The thunderstorm crashed on outside, the wind shaking the palms and stirring the huge expanse of ocean into unaccustomed violence. When she raised her lips to him again, she felt almost drugged with an answering desire which was robbing her legs of their bones, emptying her brain of anything but melting, mindless need...

On the softness of the large gold velvet chesterfield in an alcove of the sitting-room, Luc pulled her down across his lap and then pushed her flat in one urgent, seeking motion, his fingers peeling the wet silk away from her breasts. Verity gasped as he caressed the soft swell of her flesh with his hands, and then moved to repeat the action with his mouth and tongue. Convulsively, she clutched his head, her fingers blindly moving through his damp hair. She'd never felt such piercing, shattering physical pleasure, waves of it rippling through her veins. The touch of his tongue and teeth on the sensitised tips of her breasts was electric, triggering a thousand tiny shock waves through her system. She was aware, through the mists of sensation, that she was playing with fire, that this could only lead to infinite regret. But logic didn't come into this. She felt paralysed, swamped by physical and emotional responses she didn't know existed...

The crop-top was dispensed with, and she tensed inside as his hands moved lower, hungrily seeking beneath the silky skirt, caressing the slender length of her thighs and then stroking all the way up to the tight, hidden wetness which betrayed her, which answered every unspoken question Luc was silently asking...

She tensed, and then caught her lip in her teeth to stop herself from crying out, shuddering from head to toe at the reaction his exploring fingers seemed to provoke.

'I want to make love with you,' he breathed impatiently, huskily urgent as he abruptly stood up and moved to pull her up with him. 'But not here, on the sofa, like clumsy teenagers! I've waited the longest twelve months of my life for this... Come to bed, Verity...'

Wide-eyed, she stared up at him as he guided her into the bedroom, towards the green and white bed, watching him numbly as he went to close the shutters, then turned to study her flushed cheeks and defensive posture.

Fear and panic were taking over again, in the sudden respite from Luc's physical presence, and he saw it in her eyes. Now that she was free of his arms, she couldn't imagine how in the world she'd allowed things to get to this point. She was shivering all over, as reaction set in. When he came slowly towards her, she backed away so

fast that she almost tripped over the bed. Grabbing for
her apricot silk wrap, she dived into it and hugged it
around her, gritting her teeth together to stop them from
chattering.

Luc took another step towards her, and then stopped,
examining her white-faced trembling with an intensity
which reminded her of a cat examining a mouse, assessing it for entertainment value.

'Verity...'

'Luc, I'm sorry, but——'

'Verity...' His voice was deeper, with a slightly unsteady, husky note which seemed to tear her apart.

'No, Luc...I can't, I just can't, I really can't——'
Her voice rose slightly, and she caught her breath.

'Stop!' he cut in harshly, raking an abrupt hand
through his dishevelled hair. '*Dios*, Verity! Don't look
at me like that! Don't look at me as if I am some lech-
erous animal who would force you into sex!'

'Oh, please...' She couldn't help it; no amount of
will-power would prevent the tears from prickling her
eyelids, welling in her throat. She swung away from him,
hiding her face in her hands. 'Go away, Luc...please,
just go away.'

'Is that what you want?' he countered angrily, his voice
thicker, slightly ragged as he came up behind her. 'To
continue to pretend that we are *indifferent* to each other?'

'It's no good—it's just *sex*, for heaven's sake! Mechanical reactions—it doesn't mean anything,' she sobbed,
as he gently took her shoulders and turned her around,
drawing her into his arms and holding her there. Her
cheek was pressed hard against his chest, and she heard
the heavy thud of his heartbeat. There was an explosive
tension in him, far more powerful and aggressive than
hers. She sensed he was controlling himself with steely

determination. The knowledge didn't help her shattered self-esteem.

'Is that the way you really see it? This attraction between us?' he said hoarsely, finally breaking the web of tension engulfing them both. 'Isn't that the way you'd like it to be, Verity? *Just* sex? No worries about commitments?'

She pulled away, too frightened by her own weakness to let that insidious attraction begin to work again. His words held a fragment of truth, but he was wrong. There it was again, that image of a man-eating harpy. If it weren't so painfully insulting it would be almost funny. If Edward had really imparted all that intimate information about her to Luc, surely he wouldn't have made exaggerated claims about their sexual relationship? Or would he? Was that the kind of thing men told each other, to boost their standing in each other's eyes?

'Stop crying, Verity,' Luc recommended bluntly, when she didn't answer him. 'Your virtue and your *pride* remain intact, *no es verdad*? Go and wash your face and put on some clothes.'

He turned abruptly from her and left the bedroom, shutting the door with a decisive click behind him.

When he'd gone, she walked shakily into the bathroom and splashed her face with cold water, examining the flushed, swollen contours of her face and mouth with alarm and distaste.

Outside the rain was stopping, the storm dying away. The heat was as intense as ever. She slipped the apricot robe from her shoulders and flinched at the sight of the marks on her breasts, still aching and tender from the eruption of desire between herself and Luc...

How *could* she have let it get that far? How could she have lost her head to that extent? Face it, she told herself scathingly, if Luc hadn't displayed a thankfully mature preference for the comfort and privacy of a bedroom for a first sexual encounter, it would have got a great deal further.

Knowing the effect Luc had on her, how could she have been so brainless, so stupid, so easily bowled over?

As she gazed into the mirror, the answer crept into her head, stealthily staring her in the face like a feared adversary confronting her with a lethal weapon.

She loved him. She loved him so much that it terrified her. She'd loved him ever since the very first moment she saw him, jumping down from his horse at the polo match last year, just four weeks before the date fixed for her wedding to Edward...

She'd never loved Edward. He'd loved her, and that had seemed enough. She'd recognised safety, security, undemanding qualities which promised a quiet, undemanding existence. No danger, no risk to her emotions. Luc García had appeared in her life and rocked all her tidy, convenient plans with one brief, frightening glimpse of heaven...

She felt as if her carefully structured world was slowly falling apart as she went through the motions of swapping the damp, wine-stained skirt and apricot wrap for a leaf-green sundress. Shakily, her fingers refusing to function, she slipped the dress over her head and buttoned the demure scoop-neck, fastening a white leather belt at the waist. Brushing her hair into some semblance of order, she slipped her bare feet into flat white sandals, and forced herself out of the bedroom to face Luc, wishing herself a million miles away from the truth she'd just silently run up against a few minutes earlier.

Luc was on the terrace, leaning on the railing, gazing out at the darkly swelling ocean beyond the beach. The sky had cleared, and the moon was spilling arrows of silver on to the churning water.

He didn't turn round when she came out, and she stared down at the aftermath of Elliot's visit, still strewn untouched on the terrace floor. Her carefully prepared salad and chicken were swimming in a dark puddle of red wine and rain-water. As she bent to begin collecting shards of glass and crockery, Luc swung round.

'Leave it!' he said quietly. 'The maids will come over in a moment.'

'It won't take me long to clear this up,' she protested coolly.

'I said leave it!' It was an order, she recognised grimly, straightening up to meet his eyes.

'Yes, sir!' She gave a small, wry salute, eyeing him bleakly.

'Were you entertaining Grosvenor to dinner?' he queried bluntly.

'How I intended to spend my evening is *my* business,' she retorted, mustering her flagging spirits and levelling a steady, defiant look in his direction. 'And, on the subject of Elliot, I'd like to know precisely what you've done with him. The poor man was in no fit state to be dumped somewhere and told to find another hotel! He could be wandering around in a daze somewhere...'

Luc's mouth twisted drily.

'So protective,' he mocked softly. 'So I was interrupting a romantic evening for two? Though I hardly think Grosvenor could have performed very satisfactorily.'

She suppressed the urge to hit him. Her earlier display of violence had triggered unwelcome repercussions, hadn't it?

'I thought you were dining with Carli and Raoul tonight?'

'I excused myself. I wanted to talk to you.' The wry self-derision in his voice touched a chord in her and she glanced at him sharply. There was no answering tell-tale emotion in his eyes. The blue gaze was very bright and hard.

'Well, now's your chance,' she suggested lightly. As she spoke two of the maids from the hotel appeared with cleaning equipment, and they both stepped to one side.

'Have you eaten?' Luc asked her.

She shook her head, with an ironic glance at the terrace floor. 'That was my supper!'

'Come back to the hotel restaurant with me. We'll both eat there. Not here. The temptation to finish what I started might just prove too strong...' The glance he shot towards her melted her knees. 'My powers of self-control are extensive but not limitless.'

'I'm not really hungry, Luc.' How she managed to keep her voice cool and controlled, she had no idea. She felt as if she were operating on emotional auto-pilot.

'Please, Verity.' It was half-command, half-request. Swallowing hard at the unfamiliar note of persuasion in Luc's deep voice, she found herself shrugging in resignation, and nodding dumbly.

Eschewing his private suite, presumably for the same reasons, Luc led her to the table where they'd eaten on her birthday, where the sun-awning had doubled as a huge umbrella to protect the al fresco restaurant from flooding in the recent storm. Groups of guests were talking, laughing, eating and drinking. The atmosphere was light and relaxed. Some of the women greeted Luc as they arrived, their eyes lingering on him as he walked past. He was attractive to women, most women, all women, Verity reminded herself bitterly. His dark, lean height, his thick black hair and brilliant blue eyes, his rangy walk with just the faintest hint of swagger... she was hardly the first to succumb to his widely known expertise as a lover, and she wouldn't be the last...

Shivering as he held out the chair for her, she wondered if those curious female eyes following them, the eyes of experienced, married women who knew all about the whirlpool of hectic emotions Verity had almost drowned in tonight, could tell what they'd just been doing, just from looking at her?

She supposed she should be grateful for his chivalry tonight. But she felt wary, uneasy, as if she'd already given too much away, unwittingly triggered her own emotional demise. Sitting opposite Luc's broodingly controlled masculinity, with the memory of every intimate caress still burning her skin, felt like the biggest ordeal of her life so far.

Meticulous politeness controlled their every word and action as they studied the menu, discussed the variety of foods available on the island, the strong Spanish influence on the dishes available, the highlights of the day's outing. But the sight of Pablito, calm and unsmiling as he emerged from the hotel to take their order, kept her anger simmering steadily just below the surface. True, Elliot had behaved like an idiot, following her out here and then getting drunk and belligerent, but nothing, *nothing* excused the humiliation of Luc's 'heavies' interfering in that ghastly scene on her terrace, and throwing Elliot out of the hotel...

'Verity?' She realised Luc had just asked her a question and she had no idea what he'd said.

'Sorry?'

'I was saying that the hotel offers French creole dishes, from Haiti, as well as traditional Spanish. In fact there are dishes from Italy, Mexico, and Argentina as well. I can recommend the prawns with the guava and coconut sauce...'

'Anything,' she said flatly. 'You choose. I can't think straight. Why did you come to the villa tonight, Luc?'

Luc murmured something in rapid Spanish to Pablito, who nodded gravely and departed. Verity found herself caught and held in Luc's intense gaze across the glass-encased cream candle on the table.

'I came to see you,' he said quietly, 'because we need to talk.'

'Is that why you brought Pablito and his mate along with you, in case you needed a little assistance *talking*?'

Luc's eyes narrowed. 'I heard the commotion. I didn't know what the hell was going on. I thought you were being attacked!'

'Whereas that came later?' she quipped glibly, then immediately wished she hadn't as the blue gaze darkened warningly.

'If I frightened you, Verity, I am sorry,' he countered grimly, 'but I confess you have a very... unfortunate effect on my normal self-control.'

'Your normal self-control?' she echoed disbelievingly. 'Rumour has it that *seduction* is one of your main hobbies! Hardly a week goes by in England without the tabloids relating another "glamorous female" on the arm of well-known polo player Luc García, exerting that notorious Latin charm of his!'

'That worries you?' he countered softly. 'My so-called reputation with women? Greatly exaggerated, I promise you. A man like me needs only to be seen with two different women in the space of a year for the stories to circulate...'

'A man like you?' she shot back, raising her eyebrows. 'And what *is* a man like you?'

'A man without roots?' he suggested lightly, shrugging as their first course arrived. *'Pasteles en Hojas,'* Luc supplied, as she examined the tiny pies wrapped in banana leaves. 'Plantain-dough meat pies,' he added, grinning at her blank expression. 'Try them.'

'You were saying?' she persisted, tasting the pie and nodding in absent approval. 'How you're a man without roots? Why, Luc? Why are you without roots? You've got a delightful sister, and, from what Carli told me, plenty of supportive relatives out on horse ranches in Argentina, or cattle farms in northern Spain. Being rootless must be self-inflicted!'

'Yes, of course it is. Since my marriage broke up, I have deliberately avoided commitments,' he said slowly, nodding at the waiter who poured white wine into their glasses and silently disappeared again. 'And my lifestyle is also rootless. Moving from place to place, with the polo seasons across the world—it is a life which suits me, but not one which provides the...the back-up support a man needs...'

'Back-up support?' she queried mockingly. 'Oh, you mean someone to iron your shirts and put your slippers by the fire?'

Luc was silent for a moment, but he didn't laugh.

'No, that is not what I mean,' he said quietly. 'I was talking about emotional support. The kind of support you can get in a relationship where two people care, deeply, about each other. I admit that my marriage to Juliette was a non-starter in that department. However, my sister Carli assures me this unlikely state of affairs *can* exist between a man and a woman. Her own happy marriage is living proof.'

'Oh, so you're rootlessly searching the world for some paragon of virtue who measures up to this requirement?' Verity nodded gravely, unsure what was driving her to such flippant mockery when Luc appeared to be risking his pride with such personal revelations. 'Best of luck. All I can say is, I doubt it exists! No matter how secure you make your own personal little world, if you give too much of yourself you get hurt!'

The words hung between them like the tolling of a bell lingering in the humid night air.

'The way Edward would have been hurt?' Luc murmured ruthlessly, watching her face for every nuance of reaction. Verity felt her heartbeat speed up, jolting her ribcage in heavy, sick strokes. She felt consumed with the pain of loving someone who was determined to wound her. She recalled his cruel gibe earlier, about the 'psychology of guilt'. Whenever she took the risk of exposing her true feelings to Luc, he grasped the opportunity to strike a blow for his own satisfaction. He was an embittered personality. She was wasting her time, the danger she'd always sensed in her attraction towards him now magnified one hundred-fold as she recognised the enormity of his power to hurt her.

'That's not true!' she said as calmly as she could, aware of a waiter returning with the main course. 'I would never have hurt Edward! He was what I wanted, don't you understand?'

'You really believe that, don't you?' Luc said slowly, as Pablito appeared with dishes of vegetables, and remained to serve the meal expertly on to their plates. There was an impressive oval platter of red snapper stuffed with fresh local herbs, in a coconut sauce, and dishes of maize, sweet potatoes and rice. 'You believe what you had with Edward would have been enough to last you a lifetime?'

'Why not?' she defended herself shakily. 'How can you sit in judgement on my relationship with Edward?'

'A bride-to-be who could respond to another man in the way you responded that night in Florida is either fooling her prospective husband, or fooling herself. Because you wanted more. You needed more. You were just too much of a coward to admit it.'

'So you think I would have cheated on Edward to get it?'

Luc shrugged, his eyes narrowing on her flushed cheeks, and over-bright eyes.

'I have only my personal encounter with you to go on,' he pointed out cruelly.

'And you assume it was merely one of many?' She wasn't sure why she was probing Luc's opinions in this way, why she was so intent on causing herself maximum pain. Luc was playing some kind of game with her, and she made a pretence of eating the food in front of her, her appetite non-existent. 'You think I was in the habit of passionate little encounters, behind Edward's back?'

Luc leaned back in his seat, appraising her with a detached air.

'I didn't say that——'

'But you *think* it!' She put her knife and fork down, suddenly unable to pretend to eat any longer. 'You judge every female you meet by the standards of your ex-wife! Is that it?'

There was a chilling silence.

'It seems I really can't win,' he said finally, his eyes suddenly pale and brilliant with hostility. 'First I am branded a monster, accused of abandoning my sick wife because of her illness. Now I am labelled the bitter cynic who thinks all women are faithless whores. Am I right, Verity?'

'I'm sorry, Luc.' She shook her head in angry misery, her heart heavy. 'I can't stand any more of this...this cat-and-mouse game...I don't understand what you *want*!'

She prepared to stand up, but the sudden glitter of dark emotion in his eyes made her freeze for a moment, in the act of leaving the table.

'This is not a game, Verity. I want *you*.'

She stared at him, her eyes pansy-wide in her white face. The sprinkle of freckles over the bridge of her nose stood out in stark relief as she locked eyes with him in acute stress and frustration.

'You *want* me?' she echoed tautly. 'For what purpose, Luc? And for how long? Just to satisfy your ego, another female to use as a whipping-post to beat out your frustration over your failed marriage? You want to add me to the long succession of females who can boast a brief liaison with the great Luc García? No, thanks. I'm not interested...'

Luc's face was a bleak mask as he stared back at her, the cynical lines from nose to mouth seemingly etched deeper into the rugged contours of his face.

'I must try to dissuade Carli from further misguided efforts behind my back,' he mused, with soft bitterness. 'She likes to feel she is enlisting feminine understanding on my behalf. Sadly she is too naïve to realise that not all women possess her purity of spirit...'

'Purity of spirit?' Verity shot back incredulously, climbing shakily to her feet. 'You wouldn't recognise it if you hit it head-on at seventy miles an hour! A man who could try to seduce his best friend's fiancée four weeks before the wedding, and then a year later amuses himself by stirring everything up again like this? I've had enough, Luc...'

'Running away again, Verity?' The soft accusation stung like a poisoned dart.

'No, I'm *not*.'

'Why can't you face up to your own feelings?' he countered quietly. 'Why are you so afraid to sit down and talk?'

'Because you're incapable of *talking*! All you ever do is... *taunt*!' she said furiously.

'And you lock yourself away behind those fierce little defences of yours, like a maiden in an ivory tower! You hold on to your guilt like a shield,' he bit out suddenly, shooting out a steely hand to detain her as she started to turn away. 'Forget Edward, Verity, let him out of your life, stop this pretence.'

'No, you stop the pretence!' she ground out, on a half-sob, uncaring of the interested glances from their fellow diners. 'You're a hypocrite, Luc! And a sadist! I'm not sure why you dragged me out here to the Caribbean to torment me, and I'm sorry to spoil your fun, but I can't stay any longer! I'm going back to London, and, the way I feel right now, I wish I *never* had to see you again!'

Tears blurred her eyes, and she was trembling so violently with anger and frustration that it took her twice as long as usual to stumble back to the villa. In the haven of the bedroom she began blindly throwing her clothes into her suitcase, her thoughts focused only on the urgent need to escape before Luc could come and find her and take her in his arms again, and prove that her mindless physical need for him could blot out her emotional aversion...

She was tensed in readiness for his angry appearance at the door, as she packed and tidied and rang for a taxi to the airport for early the next morning.

But this time he didn't follow her.

CHAPTER EIGHT

'IT'S no good,' Sara sighed, flinging down her pen and pushing the order book aside, staring gloomily at Verity across the desk in the small bedroom they used as an office, 'I can't work out what's going on at all! That's four cancelled orders in the past week! I'm starting to feel nervous! As if there's a jinx on us or something!'

Verity chewed the tip of her thumb, her eyes on the froth of pink and white blossom on the apple tree in the garden beyond the window, her thoughts far away.

'Verity?' Sara persisted, her voice rising slightly. 'Will you just stop staring out of the window like a lovelorn teenager and *talk* to me? If orders keep vanishing into thin air the way they are at the moment, we could be in serious financial difficulty soon!'

'Sorry, Sara,' Verity said quickly, dragging her thoughts back from their wayward wanderings, and fixing a penitent gaze on her friend. They were sitting over coffee, planning their workload for the week, and the order book lay open between them, the topic of discussion illustrated graphically by the diagonal red lines deleting several of the entries. 'But please stop referring to me as a lovelorn teenager! I keep telling you, love couldn't be further from my mind!'

Sara took a thoughtful sip of coffee, and examined Verity's face and figure with critical thoroughness.

'So would you mind running through the reasons for cutting short your Caribbean visit once again for me?' she suggested sweetly. 'And explaining the fact that for the last fortnight you've been walking around like a prisoner sentenced to death, and your dress size has dropped from twelve to ten without any apparent dietary effort on your part, and the dark shadows under your eyes would do nicely for an audition for Little Nell, and that I've twice had to play personal answering machine for telephone calls from Argentina, from one Luc García you stubbornly refuse to ring back and speak to——?'

'Sara, stop it!' Verity sat up straighter, and pulled the order book towards her with a determined effort to concentrate. 'You're wildly exaggerating, as usual! And these cancelled orders aren't the end of the world. We've plenty of business lined up for May——'

'Have you rung Luc back yet?' Sara interrupted quietly.

'No! And I've no intention of doing so.'

'But you just had a "misunderstanding" while you were over there? That's how you described it. Surely a phone call wouldn't go amiss?'

'I don't want to talk to him, and I don't want to see him!'

'But he'll be back for the beginning of the English season in May,' Sara reminded her, with a touch of impatience, 'and, since we've got the contract for the catering at North Downs Polo Club, you'll have to renew acquaintance quite soon! This weekend, in fact...'

Verity stood up, her eyes fixed on her friend's unrepentant face.

'You just won't let it rest, will you?'

'What?' Sara enquired innocently.

'My so-called love-life!'

Sara stood up too, and reached to give her an impulsive hug.

'Sorry, darling! But you really are infuriating at the moment. I've never known you quite like this—not even after Edward was killed...' Sara stopped, clapping her hand to her mouth in dismay. 'Or is that *it*? Am I being horribly obtuse, Verity? Are you feeling down and depressed all over again, one year on and all that?'

Verity shook her head slowly, in guilty denial. Drawing back, she turned to fiddle with the calculator on the desk, in case Sara could read the anguish in her eyes.

She couldn't let Sara think that her present heartache was connected with Edward, because it wasn't. Not in the way Sara thought, at least...

Of course Edward's death had been deeply traumatic, but this feeling she was experiencing over Luc was a different kind of suffering, she acknowledged reluctantly. The death of someone you loved was final, a door slammed forever...something you could grieve for openly. Whereas this pain in her heart for Luc felt locked in, fenced off from prying eyes, too raw and frightening to be openly examined.

And then, she hadn't really loved Edward, had she? She could admit it to herself now. Not deeply, completely, entirely...and losing Edward had been a tragic blow, but losing Luc in the same circumstances would have felt like the end of her own life...

The secret admission was like a knife twisting in her conscience. If she felt this now, with so much space between them, such a massive gulf between them, how would she feel if she gave in to her instincts, let him close enough to cause real pain, wreak real destruction?

She closed her eyes, suddenly dizzy with the endless circling of her thoughts.

The telephone rang and Sara reached to answer it, her ready smile and brightly helpful telephone manner fading abruptly as she listened to the caller on the other end.

'I'm so sorry to hear that,' she was saying politely, 'but I quite understand. Yes, fine. Goodbye...'

'Who was that?' Verity queried, puzzled by the sudden frown of concern on Sara's face as she replaced the receiver.

'*Another* order cancellation. I've a feeling they've all come from a circle of people who know each other quite well. That was the Pennington-Crews. They don't want us to do their Silver Wedding party on the twenty-seventh...'

'Did they say why?'

Sara shook her head. They both stared at each other, the silence deepening as they absorbed the implications. Verity was the first to speak.

'Is someone deliberately making trouble, do you think?' she said slowly. 'And if so, who on earth could it be?'

Sara shrugged bleakly. 'It could just be a vindictive remark from one person, which has spread around a circle of acquaintants. You know how fast rumours fly...'

Verity had a sick feeling clutching the pit of her stomach. She stared at Sara in silence.

'Who, though? A competitor?' her friend was musing angrily, frowning fiercely out of the window at the antics of two blackbirds in the apple tree. 'Unlikely, I suppose. Even in this cut-throat business it would be fighting dirty! And I don't know of any new rivals who've set up in the last month, do you?'

Verity shook her head, winding a stray curl around her finger before pushing it jerkily back into her topknot.

'No, in fact——'

'You don't think it could be *Elliot*?' Sara asked suddenly, whirling round, her frown deepening. 'I still can't get over seeing that man in his true colours!'

Elliot had returned from the Dominican Republic and thoroughly disgraced himself by first regaling Sara with the sorry saga of his treatment in the Caribbean, and then proceeding to present Sara with the duty-free perfume and proposing that she spend the night with him by way of commiseration.

'When I told him to get on his bike, he threw a tantrum to rival a two-year-old's!' Sara recalled drily. 'To think I wasted a couple of months, at least, fantasising over him as a soul-mate! Thank heavens I saw the light! I've you to thank for that, Verity!'

'Elliot just needs to do some growing up.' Verity grimaced, still deeply embarrassed by the whole episode. 'It could be him, I suppose. But I shouldn't think it would be... He's immature, but not necessarily vindictive...'

An awful suspicion that she might know the culprit was growing heavily inside her.

Luc? Could it be Luc? He was the one who'd generously recommended them, this last year. He was the one who'd boosted their business. He was the one in the prime position to take it away again. If the spell of mental torture in the Dominican Republic had been Luc García's subtle punishment for her alleged betrayal of his friend Edward, was this, then, his revenge for her rejection of his celebrated seduction technique?

Was this Luc's arrogant displeasure for leaving him in the lurch with her hasty escape back to England?

Here, she ground to an appalled halt. Could it *really* be Luc? Would Luc attack her in this way? She shrank instinctively from the idea, and forcing herself to examine the possibility hurt so badly that it was like a stab of physical pain inside her. He might not love her, but surely he didn't *hate* her?

The last scene with him replayed itself in her head, the way it had with relentless clarity even since she'd jumped on the first available plane and fled back to England... There was an indelible image of him, leaning silently back in his chair on the hotel terrace, watching her storming at him, his face deadpan, his eyes unreadable.

She'd been so angry that she could hardly remember what she'd said before her final control flipped and she leapt to her feet. Everything had seemed to mount up to an unbearable onslaught on her emotions. His arrogance over Elliot, his taunts about her feelings for Edward and the implication that, while he might not be averse to a quick affair, she was wildly unsuitable for the role of loyal, faithful wife and partner he was apparently seeking... it had all come on top of her humiliating responses to his lovemaking, and the frightening realisation of how hopelessly she was in love with him...

He'd seemed indifferent. Uncaring whether she stayed or left. There'd been no sign of him that evening, as she lay sleepless on the bed in the villa, her nerves at screaming-point. And no sign of him when her taxi arrived early the next morning, and she disappeared to the airport. He just hadn't cared. And the two telephone calls since had doubtless been his attempts to air his displeasure at being left in the lurch over the catering he'd lined up for the end of her 'holiday'...

But surely even that didn't mean he now hated her enough to try to undermine her business? He might not have loved her, but he *had* desired her... he'd demonstrated how much, with a hunger and an urgency which took her breath away, still, whenever she thought about it.

'Verity, darling...' Sara was scanning Verity's hunted expression with a worried frown '...are you sure you're all right?'

Verity nodded stiffly, thrusting her hands into the pockets of her denims in a defensive gesture. But, to her horror, her eyes filled with tears under Sara's concerned stare. She swallowed an annoying lump in her throat.

'I'm not sure I can face bumping into Luc at this polo thing on Saturday, that's all...'

'Oh, Verity.' Sara moved to slip her arm around her shoulders, and, fighting against the ignominy of a complete breakdown, Verity twisted free and fumbled for a tissue in the sleeve of her checked blouse, avoiding her friend's eyes.

'I thought you said it was just a minor misunderstanding?' Sara pointed out, clearly shaken. 'A lover's tiff? It wasn't, obviously!'

'No.' Verity shook her head miserably, twisting away to blow her nose. 'It was a major misunderstanding... and Luc and I are *not* lovers!'

'Well, maybe not. But from the look of you, you should be! I've had you two earmarked as an item for months now. He's gorgeous, Verity! Every girl's dream. Every time I *see* the man my knees turn to water. Those piercing blue eyes and that rugged grin and all that floppy black hair!'

Verity summoned a weak smile at Sara's poetic excesses.

'I don't know why you don't snap him up! If you don't want him, just say the word—I can happily ditch

Connor and flap my eyelashes at Luc at the polo buffet on Saturday with a clear conscience!'

Connor was the latest man in Sara's life, a tawny-haired Irish restaurateur with a contagious laugh. They'd met at a party while Verity was in the Caribbean, and, since all the signs were that attraction had been instant, mutual and lasting, Verity half expected to see an engagement ring sparkling on her friend's finger any day.

'It's not funny, Sara...'

'No, it's not, is it? I don't suppose you're going to tell Aunty Sara all about it?' Sara hazarded gently.

'I can't...I can't talk about it...but thanks, anyway...' She had herself relatively under control again, picking up a set of bills for payment and extracting the cheque-book from the drawer. 'Don't worry, I'll be there on Saturday,' she added, expelling her breath shakily. 'And, in the meantime, we'd better see if we can find out who is trying to damage our business, while we still have a business to damage!'

Brave words, Verity reflected on Saturday morning, in the brilliant May sunshine, as they packed their van with tray upon tray of elaborately prepared dishes. She felt far from brave. Discounting those two perfunctory telephone calls taken by Sara, there'd been two weeks of ominous silence, following the fiasco of their last encounter, and the mere thought of seeing Luc again was tying her insides up in knots.

But she needed to see him. Tackling him about this smear campaign against Verity Lacey Catering was going to take every last vestige of courage and poise she possessed, but, in the absence of any other leads to go on, she *had* to talk to him...

At least it was a glorious day, she reflected absently, as she, Sara and four of their regular assistants worked flat out to set up the buffet in the shade of the vast green and white marquee to the side of the North Downs clubhouse.

In deference to the glamorous setting, Verity wore a short-sleeved navy silk coat-dress beneath a huge, starched white apron. At least she could discard the apron and present a smartly professional appearance when all the work was completed. With her unruly golden-brown curls forced into the tightest chignon their thickness would allow, and a light coating of tawny blusher and tan eyeshadow to disguise the strained pallor of her face, she hoped she presented the right air of restrained elegance while she worked.

Yards of trestle-tables were dressed in crisp white damask, and gradually filled with dishes of luxurious colours and textures, lavishly garnished with bunches of brilliant green parsley and watercress and red *lollo rosso*, feathery dill, and curly endive. There were fish mousses and handraised pies, prawns and caviare, soufflés and salads, terrines and *timbales*, with the centre-piece Verity's own personal triumph: six enormous fresh poached salmon, arrayed whole on a giant silver platter, garnished with rosettes of lemon mayonnaise and capers.

She was dashing out of the marquee awning in search of the operations manager, to check up on ice-buckets for the champagne, when the deep voice spoke behind her. She froze, her heart seeming to stop beating for an endless moment before racing like a piston in her chest.

'Hello, Verity.'

'Luc...' She turned round slowly, meeting that level blue appraisal with a sinking sensation in her stomach.

'At least you remember my name,' he mocked softly, his eyes roaming over her, his expression guarded.

She stared at him helplessly, struggling with her perverse reaction at the sight of him after two long weeks of absence . . . He looked as if he'd been out on the field, putting in some practice before this afternoon's match. In open-neck blue polo shirt, white breeches and tan boots, he exuded raw masculinity and glowing good health.

Those frantic, devastating few minutes in the Villa Laguna the night before she left came flooding back into her mind, and she felt hot all over, and freshly angry. Was she mad? How could she feel so *overwhelmed* by him, after all that had happened, after the way he'd behaved, and above all after what she suspected he was doing to her business? Biting her lip, she steeled herself, blinking at the hard glitter of his stare.

'How are you, Verity?' There was something about the way he was looking at her which was taking her breath away. 'You look thinner. Have you been dieting?'

'No! Luc, I'm rather busy,' she said unsteadily, striving for calm. On closer inspection, the glow of good health masked a leaner, hollower contour to his cheeks, and shadows under his eyes. 'Is there something specific you wanted?'

Luc's eyes narrowed, and a faint gleam of bitter humour touched his mouth.

'Yes. There is. There's something I want very badly from you, Verity. But that can wait for a more appropriate moment. Right now I want to know why you didn't return my telephone calls.'

'Luc, for heaven's sake, what was the point?' she protested coolly, her heart beginning to pound at the ominous drawl in his voice. 'We have absolutely nothing left to say to each other!'

'I disagree.'

'You would!' she shot back, goaded for a second out of her precarious calm. 'But that just sums it all up, doesn't it? We disagree on just about everything there is to disagree on!'

Luc opened his mouth to reply just as Sara came up to join them, short blonde hair blowing in the breeze, green eyes darting curiously from one to the other.

'Hi, Luc!' She lifted a cheek to be kissed, flicking Verity a stern look. 'You look well!'

The smile he gave her was one of his slow-burning ones which Verity had witnessed so many times, yet still caused her to twist up inexplicably inside whenever it was aimed at someone else.

'So do you,' Luc told Sara lightly, 'and so does the buffet. You can spare Verity for a while, can't you? I need to talk to her.'

'Sorry, I'm far too busy now,' Verity said flatly, eyeing the constant hive of activity surrounding them. The club was preparing to receive its first distinguished guests, and a band was tuning up outside the marquee, with a combination of brass instruments and banjos, lending a carnival air to the proceedings in their white trousers, brilliant green and gold blazers, and straw boaters with emerald ribbons.

Luc was eyeing her from head to toe, his blue gaze narrowed intently on her mutinous expression. Reaching to tilt her chin up towards him, he said quietly, 'Half an hour, Verity. Come and have a drink with me in the bar.'

'I don't have half an hour to spare, Luc!' she snapped, goaded into anger by the insidious effect of his touch.

She jerked her face away. 'I'm here in a professional capacity. I'm here on business! And frankly, with the way things have been going recently, I'm lucky to still *have* a business!'

People were brushing by them, pausing to greet Luc. A girl in a short black skirt and white silk jacket stopped to fling enthusiastic arms around his neck, shiny Titian hair cascading down her back as she reached up to him, kissing him hard on the cheek, assuring him in a husky voice how pleased she was to see him back in England.

Verity cast around desperately for an escape route, berating herself inwardly for her cowardice.

'What's been going on?' Luc was querying, having brushed off the redhead with a coolly polite greeting and another of those devastating smiles. He was glancing quickly from Verity to Sara. 'What do you mean, you're lucky to have a business?'

'I mean that, just recently, *someone* has been having lots of fun stirring up trouble for us,' she flashed back coldly. 'Ever since I came back from my abortive stay in your fancy Caribbean hotel, in fact...'

As soon as the words were out she clenched her teeth over her lip in horror. But it was too late to retract, the statement hung between them, with all its unspoken implications and inferences...

She dared not look at Sara, but she could sense that her friend had frozen into appalled disbelief.

Her eyes met Luc's, and she flinched inwardly at the glacial expression she encountered.

'Precisely what are you saying, Verity?'

Luc's eyes were narrowed blue slits in the sunshine.

'I'm talking about rumours and cancelled orders... What exactly *have* you been doing this past fortnight?' she challenged angrily, but as she blurted out the accusation she knew, in her heart, that it couldn't be Luc. What was she *doing*? She was hurting herself more than she was hurting Luc... A wave of heat engulfed her, and she took a gulp of air into her lungs to sustain herself against the expected attack.

As she watched him, aghast at her own stupidity, a tinge of angry colour darkened his face, and then receded, leaving him paler beneath his tan.

'During this past fortnight?' Luc echoed slowly, grimly. 'Do I need an alibi, Verity? Very well, during this last fortnight, I have been attending to personal matters...'

Growing anger was drawing the rugged features of his face into a chilling mask which made her clench her fists involuntarily at her sides.

'I have been visiting my ex-wife, my ex-father-in-law, my family in Argentina, playing polo, and, for some inexplicable reason, wishing I was with you!'

'Luc, I——'

'And now let me be sure that I understand you, Verity,' he went on, in a low, taut voice, his accent thickening in the smouldering heat of his anger. 'You are accusing me of trying to sabotage your business? You are serious?'

'All I know is, business has been mysteriously disappearing this last month... frankly, we're lucky to still have *this* contract!' she shot back shakily, thrown into painful confusion by the dark fury of his reaction.

'And, naturally, you thought of me?' Luc drawled coldly. 'The obvious candidate for such underhand practices? *Muchas gracias*, Verity! Your trust is infinitely touching!'

'Why *should* I trust you?' she said heatedly, her own colour rising. 'Give me one good reason!'

Luc took hold of her forearm, pulling her abruptly towards him. His touch seemed to burn her skin. Subjected to the full onslaught of his glittering gaze, she felt her control slipping dangerously.

'Because without trust the rest is a waste of time!' he stated bleakly, the raw conviction in his eyes boring into hers with such intensity that she could only gaze at him in distraught silence.

'Luc, neither of us thinks for a minute that you're to blame!' Sara cut in quietly. 'Verity's not thinking too straight at the moment...'

'Is that so?' he drawled, softly mocking.

'It's just that we're both so worried,' Sara went on hastily, with a warning glare at Verity. 'If we don't find out who's causing trouble for us soon, our reputation will be ruined, and it could be really difficult getting it back again!'

'Leave it to me,' Luc said curtly, his glance very bright and hostile on Verity's white face. 'I will make some enquiries. Whoever it is will wish they'd picked another victim.'

'It's been an interesting talk,' he added with a politely chilling finality which made Verity's stomach sink even further. 'Now, if you'll both excuse me, I need to speak to my grooms...'

In shattered silence, she watched him stride off towards the stable-blocks, his tall frame moving with its customary lithe grace. She stared after him until he disappeared out of sight around the corner of the clubhouse, and then she closed her eyes with a wave of frustrated misery which threatened to totally annihilate her precarious self-control.

'Frankly, Verity, if you weren't my oldest friend and business partner, I'd strangle you right now, with my bare hands!' Sara told her grimly, linking arms and almost frog-marching her towards the clubhouse bar. 'But, since you *are* my oldest friend, I'd better buy you a stiff brandy before all hell breaks loose in the marquee! Come on...'

Verity wasn't sure how she survived the next few hours. With a professional smile fixed on her lips, surrounded by the champagne-sipping *glitterati* of the polo world, she somehow managed to talk and laugh with various groups, keeping an eye on the quantities of food as guests came and went with plates piled high, but she was conscious only of Luc's presence, moving among the same people but keeping a cool distance from her, as if they were total strangers.

'The polo's starting, are you coming to watch?' Sara came up beside her, worriedly examining Verity's pale, set face as they bumped into each other during the proceedings. 'Are you OK, love? You look done-in!'

'I'm OK...'

'The sooner you and Luc reach some sort of truce, the happier the atmosphere around here!'

'Truce?' Verity echoed bitterly. 'No chance! After my little performance this morning, Luc will have finally crossed me off the list of pursuable females...'

'What *possessed* you to accuse him like that?' Sara couldn't help herself from asking, shaking her head in grim wonderment. Outside, the hearty male voice over the Tannoy was announcing the imminent start of a charity match, thanking the sponsors for their generosity, even mentioning the wonderful buffet and praising Verity Lacey Catering by name.

'I don't know what possessed me—lunacy, maybe?' Verity gave her a wan smile, and put a hand to her forehead, squeezing her eyes shut for a moment. 'It just came tumbling out! The stupid thing is, I really didn't think it could be him! But I've really ruined everything now. The principle of *trust* was at stake, and I've well and truly blown my chances!'

'Blown your chances?' Sara teased gently. 'But I thought you said there was no question of romance between you two anyway? Are you finally admitting that you *do* care about Luc?'

'Oh, I care,' Verity confirmed huskily, turning away to take a long, shaky breath. 'I care about him more than I've ever cared about anyone in my life, Sara! I love the wretched man to distraction. I fell in love with him the first moment I saw him, even before Edward was killed, and he utterly despises me for it! Isn't that the biggest joke you ever heard?'

CHAPTER NINE

OUTSIDE in the brilliant sunshine, the eight players were cantering on to the field, and spectators were taking their seats alongside. Glamorous wide-brimmed hats, short silky suits and field-glasses were much in evidence, and many of the guests were taking their glasses of champagne with them.

It was warm, a perfect May Saturday, with a gentle breeze fluttering the blue and white bunting around the clubhouse, and flapping the sponsor's advertising flag above the marquee. Verity was so preoccupied, as she followed Sara to a seat in front of the bar terrace, that it took her a while to register what the voice on the loudspeaker was saying.

Then her cheeks burned as she realised, incredulously, that her own progress towards her seat was the subject of the loudspeaker commentary! She was being pinpointed by the jocular voice on the loudspeaker as Miss Verity Lacey herself, the creator of those mouthwatering dishes everyone had just enjoyed, the hazel-blonde in the navy silk dress, preparing to take her seat to watch the charity match alongside her partner, Miss Sara Carlton.

A sporadic ripple of applause pattered around the field, and Verity dived for the sunglasses in her bag, excruciatingly embarrassed, gluing a smile on to her lips in anguished self-consciousness.

'Did you put them up to this?' she hissed at Sara, thrusting the sunglasses on to her nose.

Sara shook her head, crossing her legs beneath her green floral dress with a wry glance at the players out on the field. 'But I think I can guess who did. His first move to restore our reputation, possibly?'

She was still shooting odd, curious glances at Verity, clearly dumbfounded by the statement she'd heard a few minutes earlier. Sara had never known what happened between Luc and Verity in Florida. Now that it was finally out in the open, Verity found she was past caring whether Sara knew her guilty secret or not. She'd clammed it up inside her for a year. Giving it a healthy airing would do no harm. Or for 'healthy airing' substitute 'last rites', she reflected bitterly. Her well-suppressed yearning for Luc García would need to be put humanely to sleep, after today's fiasco...

· She focused slowly on Luc's muscular figure, motionless on his dark bay horse in the centre of the field. He looked like a warrior awaiting battle, she thought involuntarily, with his horse reined-in under ruthless control, his stick resting against his shoulder like a weapon. She found herself absorbing the details with an almost photographic attention, from the intricate helmet, wrist-bands, knee-pads, straps and spurs of his armour to the immaculately plaited mane and tail and blue-bandaged legs of his horse, right down to the striped *mandille* beneath the saddle.

Was this public announcement his doing? Putting the spotlight on her deliberately to embarrass her? A cryptic, tongue-in-cheek signal to emphasise his innocence, possibly?

Dry-mouthed, she forced herself to look on the positive side. It *was* a boost for the company. In any other circumstances, she'd have been delighted. As it was, it only deepened her feeling of guilt. Made her feel ten times worse. Which, she felt quite certain, was Luc's intention...

The match began, and the air became filled with the beat of hoofs and the swish of canes, and the hard rap of bamboo. She watched, mesmerised, as she'd been last year that fateful day at the Palm Springs club in Florida. Luc usually played with stylish aggression, standing high in the saddle as he galloped, leaning out at reckless angles.

Today he seemed charged with even more ruthless drive than usual. To Verity, it looked as if he was channelling the icy fury she'd provoked into the physical action on the field. The spinning turns he executed looked even more impossible, his strategic diversion of his opponents more hostile. There seemed to be a cold anger in the way he raised his stick in a ruthless, soaring arc before cracking it down in punishing contact with the ball.

'He's impressive,' Sara murmured lightly, as the dust flew from the dry grass of the field, and the grim-faced players galloped past. 'You have to admit it.'

Verity nodded numbly. 'Yes, he is...' Inside, she felt as if she were slowly turning to stone. Half-time brought the traditional treading of the divots, and Verity walked the field with Sara, wishing she could make her escape. Sara was talking to her about something, and she was giving non-committal murmurs in response, but she wasn't really listening, inwardly plunged into turmoil.

Could she plead pressure of work, and disappear into the marquee to supervise the tail-end of the buffet? Sara would know it was an excuse. Everything was under control, and she knew it. And for some illogical reason she felt compelled to see it through to the bitter end. It was like a reluctant compulsion—knowing Luc's team were going to win, but driven to watch them do so. The inner emotional tug-of-war was beginning to give her a headache. There was only so much more of this she could take. She didn't really *want* to watch any polo match, let alone one in which Luc played such a starring role. The thumbscrew and rack would be acceptable alternatives...

The redhead in the white silk jacket was over by the horse-lines, talking to Luc, she noticed out of the corner of her eye. Luc was drinking mineral water out of a large bottle, one arm loosely slung over his horse's neck, and saying something which made the girl laugh in delight. Verity averted her eyes quickly, but not before Luc had spotted her and slowly lowered the bottle, gazing at her with narrow-eyed concentration which sent her pulse-rate abruptly soaring.

The second half of the match was almost a *fait accompli*. Amid excited shouts from the crowd, and the enthusiastic commentator on the Tannoy yelling, 'They're running away with it!' Luc's team thundered predictably towards victory.

Verity sat dutifully watching, her head pounding. The sun felt warm on the back of her head. She felt as if she were sinking into an almost dreamlike trance. The effects of the brandy Sara had forced her to drink, she decided ruefully. Her friend had seemed convinced brandy was the cure-all for the occasion, whereas nothing could take away this empty, bleak feeling in her heart ...

She'd just closed her eyes, to ease her headache, when Sara's involuntary intake of breath made them fly open again just in time to watch, seemingly in slow motion, as a player from the losing team charged Luc's horse, with reckless disregard for the rules, and Luc was thrown violently from the saddle to land on the dry turf with a thud as devastating as the one in her nightmare.

Frozen for a split second, her throat constricted, her heart pounding so fast that she thought it might burst in her chest, she felt a blurred confusion in her mind. Edward's accident, the recurring nightmare ... she must be dreaming, this couldn't be happening again ...

But Luc lay on the field, motionless, the other players circling him on horseback in that odd, ritualistic style of polo players when a team member is hurt. Pure, cold terror rose in her throat. She was catapulted to her feet, scarcely aware of her actions, incoherent with fear. The voice she heard screaming Luc's name was her own, until nightmare and reality became indistinguishable, and she was falling into the spinning darkness which had haunted her dreams for the last twelve months ...

She was half sitting, half lying in the reclined front seat of a car when she opened her eyes, and Luc was leaning over her, frowning intently, concern in every line of his body.

'*Luc*?' She blinked up at him groggily, then opened her eyes wider. Her head throbbed, in fact her forehead felt as if it had been hit with a large rock, but in a pure, soaring wave of relief she hazily digested the fact that, far from lying on the polo field with a broken neck, Luc appeared to be fit, alive and all in one piece.

'Are you all right, Verity?' he queried abruptly, anxiety clouding his eyes.

'Yes... I only fainted!' She struggled to sit upright, then felt a wave of nausea rise up inside her. Paper-white, she pressed her hand to her mouth, and Luc hurriedly reached into the back of the open sports car for a bottle of water.

'Luc... I feel sick...'

'It's all right. Put your head down, between your legs...' He thrust her forward, and she gasped and gulped in air, registering with dim relief that the nausea was receding as the blood rushed to her head.

'It's OK... I'm better now,' she managed to say, shivering as he let her go. 'I feel an idiot! You're the one who had the spectacular fall, and here you are, treating me like an invalid!'

'Falling off horses is a regular occurrence in polo,' he told her wryly, raking her face with a tinge of relief as he saw some of the colour returning. 'I was winded, that is all. No broken bones, even.'

'I thought...' Her voice choked off. Suddenly she didn't trust herself to tell him what she'd thought as she saw him fall. If she tried, she was terrified of bursting into tears, and she didn't think she could face the humiliation of explaining them away.

'You thought of Edward?' he prompted, his voice managing somehow to be harsh yet gentle at the same time. 'You thought that history might be repeating itself, Verity?'

She nodded slowly. 'Something like that.'

Luc straightened up, his eyes hard to read as he gazed down at her musingly.

'Is your vision all right?' he asked with a wry twist of his lips. 'Can you remember what day it is?'

Frowning at him, she nodded again. 'I'm totally *compos mentis*! What on earth is all the fuss about?'

'Sara thought you hit your head on the back of a seat as you fell. I managed to persuade her that I would take care of the situation.'

The redhead in the white jacket had detached herself from a small crowd of people near the polo field, and was making her way across to them, winding her way through the serried ranks of Porsches, BMWs and Mercedes in the car park.

She smiled possessively from Luc to Verity. 'Revived the damsel in distress?' she queried. 'What was it, darling?' she added, turning long emerald-green eyes on Verity. 'Touch too much brandy? Is everything all right now? You're wanted in the bar, Luc! Victory champagne is about to be drunk!'

Verity was opening her mouth to retort, when Luc said softly, 'Hopefully, everything's fine. Or it may be, when I drive Verity home.'

Without altering the deadpan set of his face, he bent and kissed Verity slowly, and lingeringly, on the mouth. When he straightened up again, the smile had frozen on the other girl's lips.

'Fine. I'll tell them not to wait for you, shall I?' she said stiffly, swinging away with a toss of her head before flouncing off across the grass, fury in every elegant line of her body.

Putting a hand to her lips, Verity stared at Luc, her cheeks burning.

'Do me a favour in future?' she whispered furiously. 'When you tire of your current lover *don't* use me as a convenient method of ridding yourself of her!'

'*Dios*!' Luc muttered, reaching to pull her to her feet and into the taut steel of his arms. 'Are you crazy? That girl means *nothing*, I cannot even remember her *name*, Verity...'

She began to protest at such a sweepingly arrogant statement, but Luc covered her mouth again with hungry urgency, his lips moving on hers with such pent-up desire, her brain went blank. When he released her slightly, she stared at him in growing despair. She felt like a poor swimmer fighting a lethally strong current.

'Where's Sara?' she managed to whisper, making one last effort to restore normality to what threatened to become another dreamlike trance. 'What happened when I fainted, Luc?'

'I got up, dusted myself down,' he told her, tilting a finger beneath her chin which revealed a slightly unsteady hand, 'then discovered I was no longer the centre of attention. My horse received a cut from the collision. I came off the field to hand her over to my groom to change horses, and then saw who was stealing my limelight!'

'You didn't finish the match?'

He gave an almost imperceptible shake of his head.

Verity caught her lip between her teeth, shivers of reaction beginning to result from the close contact of their bodies, where Luc still held her crushed against him. He tightened his arms around her, then glanced down at his sweat-damp polo gear, his dusty and dishevelled appearance.

'I am ruining your dress,' he pointed out huskily.

'I'll send you the cleaning bill,' she whispered, a smile trembling on her mouth. 'Oh, Luc, I was so frightened. It was like a dream I've been having, these last twelve months... a nightmare. One that's made me feel even more guilty—a dream where it was you, and not Edward, who was killed that day...'

'Wishful thinking?' Luc suggested, his gaze darkening on her white face.

'*No*!' The anguished response was jerked from her. 'Never! I don't think I could *live* if you died...'

The words hung, emotive and helplessly revealing, and Verity stared at him, aghast, then squeezed her eyes tightly shut to blot out the narrowed hardness of the blue gaze trained down on her face.

'*Verity*?' She felt him shake her gently, and opened her eyes to see the taut mask of his face, the kindling hunger in his eyes, and with a surge of panic she went on quickly,

'And that's the trouble! That's the kind of... of *dependence* I can't handle...'

'Get into the car,' he ordered grimly, propelling her back into the passenger-seat and reaching to strap her in with controlled precision. 'You are rambling like a simpleton! I'll drive you straight to Casualty. The doctors can check for concussion.'

'Luc, I am *not* concussed!' she told him furiously, twisting round in her seat to glare at him as they pulled out of the car park and on to the open road. 'Don't be ridiculous.'

'Prove it,' he suggested huskily, the glance he gave her devastating her defences. 'Try making a few sane, honest statements to convince me, *cara*.'

Balling her fists in frustration, she closed her eyes, gritting her teeth. The open sports car was a maroon Aston Martin, and Luc was gunning it along the country lanes at a speed which was blowing her hair loose from its already dishevelled chignon, and effectively blowing the cobwebs from her brain at the same time.

How *could* she have blurted out what she'd said? Telling him she couldn't live if he'd died? The after-effects of fainting *must* have addled her brain...

'Well?' Luc prompted calmly. 'I'm waiting.'

'All right, what do you want me to say? My name is Verity Lacey,' she began indignantly, 'I'm twenty-three years old. I share a ground-floor flat in Wimbledon with Sara Carlton, who is also my partner in my catering business. Today is the first Saturday in May, I've just done the catering for the North Downs Polo Club charity match, and...'

'And you are in love with me.'

She stopped, holding her breath, suddenly not daring to look at him.

'And you are the most arrogant, conceited, self-assured *overbearing* man I have ever met,' she finished up in a quiet fury.

'But you love me, Verity.' The deep voice held a mixture of amusement, resignation, and some other emotion which made her cheeks grow hot, and her stomach melt.

Collecting her shattered wits, she realised they'd entered the outskirts of London. Luc's precision handling

of the car in the hectic city traffic was strangely reassuring. But she shook her head in angry denial.

'No, I don't! I don't even *like* you! You...you taunt
me over Edward, even though you were equally to blame,
you accuse me of planning to cheat on him, then of
stringing *Elliot* along just because he's rich...no, Luc,
I don't love you, and you most definitely don't love me!
Frankly I doubt if you know how to love *any* woman!
Juliette hurt you badly, and since then you've just played
the field! With a cynical eye for the main chance!'

The car turned quietly down a cobbled mews street in
an exclusive area, and drew up outside a tall brick
building, with a black front door flanked by two bay
trees in oak tubs. Breathless from her outburst, she
turned reluctantly to look at Luc, and found him re-
garding her with a level, intent gaze which took her
breath away.

'What are we doing here?' she queried shakily, as he
climbed out and came round to open her door. 'I thought
you said you were driving me home...'

'This is my home, in London.'

He ushered her into a square oak-floored hall, and
then into a large sunny room overlooking a walled
garden. She stared out through the windows. A sun-
bleached wooden bench stood beneath a brilliant scarlet
japonica trained against one of the old brick walls,
among a mass of overblown tulips, their petals already
dropping on to the grass...

'The garden needs some attention.' Luc followed her
gaze. 'I only got back from Argentina late last night. I
think the gardener is on holiday...'

'No, the garden looks lovely.'

'Sit down,' he suggested calmly. 'Would you like a drink?'

'Luc, I think I'd better go back to my flat in Wimbledon...'

'Tea? Coffee? My housekeeper has the day off today, but I can brew a very acceptable pot of English tea.'

'Thank you. Tea would be...nice.' Verity expelled her breath unsteadily, and thrust a hand through her wildly tousled curls. 'May I use your bathroom?'

The blue gaze narrowed assessingly. 'If you promise not to run away again.'

'I'm not feeling up to running anywhere at the moment,' she said tonelessly, following his directions to the bathroom while he went to make the tea.

Her ashen face stared back from the mirror, the freckles on her nose starkly accentuated, her hair tangled in a golden aureole around her head and shoulders. Despairingly, she rinsed her face and did her best to tame her hair with the small brush in her shoulder-bag.

Her heart was beating three times as fast as normal, and her palms felt damp with nerves. Fighting a very real urge to make a bolt for it, she forced herself to return to the sitting-room, on legs which felt detached from the rest of her body.

Luc wasn't there. Too agitated to sit down, she wandered round, staring at the oil-paintings on the walls. Horses, mainly, and some bold Picasso-style flower paintings. The chairs and sofas were striped satin, in muted shades of dark crimson and silver-grey. The furniture was antique, mainly walnut, its golden glow giving the room a casual, informal feel. Books lined one wall. She walked slowly along beside the shelves. Everything seemed to be there, she registered distantly, from the latest bestsellers to the latest literary prize winners, leather-bound classics, foreign authors...Luc appeared to be well and widely read...

'Here we are...' Luc came across the room with a tray, and put it down on a low coffee-table. 'Milk, no sugar. Right?'

She nodded wordlessly. What was she doing here? This could only end in agonising pain and disappointment, in more bitter recriminations.

Luc passed her the tea, taking his own black with lemon. Facing her across the table, he leaned back in his chair and watched her take a reviving sip of the hot liquid, stretching long, booted legs in front of him and rubbing a hand over his face. Suddenly, he looked exhausted. Her heart contracted fiercely. She put down her cup, and met his eyes squarely.

'Are you all right, Luc? You look really tired...I can get a taxi home from here. There's no need to worry about me.'

'You think not?' There was a bleak intensity in his gaze.

Swallowing convulsively, she took a deep breath to boost her courage, facing him with stiff formality.

'Luc...I apologise for implying that you could in any way be responsible for the...the recent fall-off in orders,' she began unsteadily. 'It was unforgivable of me. I'm sorry...I was just so angry and confused to see you again, I wanted to lash out and hurt you——'

'Forget it. It is not important,' Luc interrupted coolly, the blue gaze narrowing speculatively on her flushed cheeks, his expression suggesting that he was gleaning a great deal more from her words than a mere acknowledgement of his innocence. 'I have an idea who may be behind it all. I have ruffled a few feathers this last couple of weeks. I finally severed all remaining financial ties with my ex-wife, and her father. In doing so I made it clear to Federico de Santana that his emotional blackmail can no longer continue. Juliette's infidelity destroyed our marriage. A sense of responsibility for her was a luxury I could no longer afford, since I intended to come to England in hot pursuit of Miss Verity Lacey of Verity Lacey Catering...'

She opened her mouth, then stopped, her heart thudding. Panic was assailing her, like an invisible net closing in on her. Putting trembling hands to her face and rubbing her eyes, she stared blankly at Luc's composed expression.

'You... you think Juliette's father could have spread some rumours? To... to try to undermine me?'

He shrugged. 'It's possible. Don't worry, Verity. Trust me. I will deal with it.'

She did trust him, she admitted with a jolt. She trusted him more than she realised... Somehow she had the impression that Luc García would prove a daunting adversary for anyone, even someone as reputedly rich and powerful as his ex-father-in-law.

She gazed at him, questions gathering in her head in a jumble of urgent curiosity, overriding her caution.

'You said you intended to come to England in ''hot pursuit'' of me? And yet you were *foul* to me in Puerto Plata,' she protested with shaky disbelief. 'And anyway, two whole weeks have passed since I left...'

There was a gleam of grim humour in his eyes at her protest.

'It seemed a long time to you?' His mouth twisted wryly. 'To me, too.'

She flushed slightly, biting her lip, and he gave a sharp sigh, and raked an abrupt hand through his dark hair.

'If I treated you badly when you came to the Dominican Republic...I confess it was because I was trying to come to terms with the way I felt about you, and a quantity of bad feelings from the past made it...difficult for me. My experience with Juliette made me...wary. To be truthful, I was afraid of showing my feelings too soon. When that fool Grosvenor turned up, I convinced myself you weren't worth the sleepless nights. When you both disappeared from the island that morning, I thought at first you might have gone together. I nearly went crazy.'

Luc's gaze was shuttered beneath narrowed lids as he watched her stunned reaction.

'But we *didn't* leave together, Luc! And you must have realised there was nothing between Elliot and me.'

He nodded slowly. 'Yes...you'd made that clear enough. But jealousy plays cruel tricks, Verity. And so does guilt. My feelings about Edward also made me treat you badly, *cara*. He was a very good friend. He was supportive and loyal when I was going through hell over Juliette. My reactions on meeting his beloved fiancée last year in Florida were not exactly guaranteed to give me an easy conscience! His death so soon afterwards drove the wedge of guilt deep into my heart.'

'Oh, Luc...'

'But I've done a great deal of thinking, this past fortnight,' he went on slowly, taking a brief drink of his tea. 'These last two weeks have felt like two years. When I finally conquered my pride enough to ring you, you didn't return my calls. I confess pride then stopped me from jamming the lines between Argentina and England.

Pride, and the need for a little time to get everything clear in my mind.' His mouth twisted wryly. 'I wanted very badly to come to England, to see you straight away, but also I wanted to sort out my personal affairs, as well as my own feelings. I did not want any complications to stand in the way...I wanted to sweep the slate clean. Cut out the dead wood. Make room for the priorities in my life. And now I know exactly what I want, Verity.'

'Don't, Luc...don't say it...'

She reached forwards blindly to pick up her teacup, her fingers shaking, the panic-net tightening around her. Avoiding Luc's penetrating gaze, she took a sip of tea and willed her unruly emotions under control.

'Verity, can we stop sipping tea like polite strangers?' he said in a low, measured voice. She had the impression he was reining in his temper. Lowering her eyes, she tried to calm her wayward pulse-rate.

'Sipping tea like polite strangers is better than making wild statements neither of us really mean,' she said quietly, after a long silence stretched out between them. 'Seeing you fall this afternoon...I'm afraid I felt rather...over-emotional. I said some rather wild things...I'm sorry.'

Luc was on his feet in one fluid, decisive movement. He took the cup from her hand, and jerked her up with him.

'*Basta*! Enough!' he said softly. 'We have talked too much—I have to show you how I feel about you, Verity...' His voice thickened as he raked his hands along the narrow expanse of her back and then cupped her face with a shudder of impatience. 'And to show you how you feel about me...'

*   *   *

She knew she should argue, fight, resist, but the physical sensation of Luc's body moulded against hers and the husky warmth in his deep voice sapped her resistance. And the emotional upheaval of the afternoon seemed to have robbed her of her will-power. Common sense, the danger of lowering her guard with a man like Luc García, all the logical considerations deserted her. Even her pride failed to come to her rescue.

Luc's sudden assault on her senses was far from gentle, but inside her a bewildering, astonishing capitulation, which she could only assign to the fright of thinking he was dead, sent her arms up round his neck, and her lips seeking his with unabashed hunger.

Her fingers threaded into the thick dampness of his black hair, still plastered to his head where he'd perspired beneath the hard hat in the frenetic physical exertion of the match. Shivering, mindless with need, she leaned against him, her knees turning to rubber.

Sensing her response, Luc deepened the kiss, his tongue probing hers, his hands smoothing her body through the fine silk dress and then circling to cup the heavy jut of her breasts, his thumbs grazing the tight peak of her nipples, growing more urgent as he tugged the buttons of her dress apart to caress the warm satin of her skin beneath.

Verity caught her breath chokingly in her throat, all defences gone. The touch of his fingers on her breasts triggered such a rapturous wantonness that suddenly it didn't matter if loving him would destroy her peace of mind... the truth was that her peace of mind had vanished the first moment she met him, and as long as she denied this burning, smouldering desire inside her she could never regain it...

'Love me, Luc.' The soft words were whispered, torn from her involuntarily, part of her hating herself for her stupidity, the other part no longer caring. 'I want you to make love to me...now, please...'

'Verity...' The soft groan of desire was wrenched from him, but he loosened his hold on her, stepping back slightly to gaze down at her flushed face and unfocused eyes as she clung to his shoulders. His eyes were darker, a glimmer of rueful amusement mingling with the sexual hunger.

'And I want it too, *cara*,' he teased unevenly, his smile melting her completely. 'But I need a shower—how you can find me irresistible, smelling of stale sweat and dust, I cannot imagine!'

She stiffened, a wave of shyness and self-consciousness returning, but with a short laugh Luc pulled her to him, and before she realised what he intended he had swung her into his arms, and was carrying her purposefully upstairs, through a large, sunny gold and white bedroom and into a pine-panelled bathroom.

'Luc, put me down, for heaven's sake...let me out of here!' she protested, pink in the face as he lowered her to the floor and smiled his slow-burning smile at her.

'Ah, no! It is too dangerous to let you go while I shower,' he said lightly, as he flicked on the tap in the cubicle and began to rip off his clothes with a masculine self-assurance which electrified her. 'So we will shower together...'

'Luc, *no*!' Shattered by the maelstrom of reactions to Luc's muscular nakedness, she flinched as he began expertly removing her own clothes, but, as each article was stripped off with a triumphant kiss, his blithe lack of inhibition became contagious. Verity finally found herself hauled beneath the warm jets of water, half laughing, half protesting, and then utterly spellbound all over again as he proceeded to soap them both with such cunning expertise that she was melting in his arms as he helped her out and wrapped a huge white bath-sheet around her shoulders.

From being tense and self-conscious, Verity felt as if she'd showered naked with Luc every day of her life. There was something strong, healthy, infectiously captivating about his matter-of-fact attitude to their bodies.

He was so supremely confident, his male arrogance was so undentable, and yet the laughter in his eyes warmed right through to the centre of her heart.

'Come to bed,' he said huskily, laughter abruptly dying from his eyes as he reached to part the folds of the towel and drew her hard against his still-damp body. 'I want you so badly, I think I will die if I don't have you, *cara*...'

A lump in her throat, she pressed her face against the rough mat of hair on his chest, and shuddered convulsively.

'I love you, Luc,' she whispered despairingly. 'I love you so much...'

She was crying, she realised dimly, as he scooped her up once more and took her to the wide bed in the centre of the bedroom.

'Why the tears?' he teased softly. 'I also love you...'

'You do?' The sudden rush of dizzy happiness nearly drowned her. 'Truly?'

'Truly. I will show you how much, Verity.' There was a brilliant gleam of victory in his eyes. 'So, you see, there is no need to cry.'

With the final, joyous reassurance of his words, the spark of sexual desire kindling between them abruptly flared into a conflagration, so fierce and all-consuming that there was no time for further words or assurances.

Verity shimmered into growing awareness beneath the hard, unfamiliar contours of Luc's body. Every inch of her responded dramatically to the slightest touch or caress. Luc's skin felt cool beneath her increasingly daring fingers, as she explored the sinews and hollows of his back, shoulders, thighs, growing more confident as she hazily registered the powerful response she could provoke in him.

There was a moment of panic, when her choked, muffled gasps of pleasure fanned the flames too fast and Luc's desire eclipsed her own and his control began to slip, but he seemed to know, slowing things down with lazy, drugging kisses and tantalising exploration, until she opened to him in blind, wild urgency, pulling him down against her and wrapping herself around him in astonished rapture.

'I have wanted this for so long...' he murmured, huskily triumphant as he stroked sensitive hands the length of her body and lifted her hips to meet the powerful, masculine thrust of possession. 'Ah, Verity...'

Her quick, tense gasp was forced back into her throat as his mouth covered hers, his tongue moving against hers, but he slowed again, feeling the sudden, uncontrollable trembling of her limbs, levering himself away a fraction to stare down into her white face with growing, incredulous understanding.

'You're a virgin?' he whispered, his narrowed gaze brilliant on her face. 'Verity, *chica*, *no es posible...*'

'It doesn't matter, does it?' she whispered fiercely, holding his rigid shoulders more tightly, willing the idiotic shivering to stop. 'Everyone is a virgin to start with! Does it make any difference?'

Luc's response was half-laugh, half-groan.

'No, *cara*, it makes no difference at all,' he assured her with wry, tender irony, 'except to make me feel the most privileged man on this earth...' And he lowered his mouth to kiss her again, hungry, soothing, devouring kisses, as if to feed from her very soul, blotting out everything else until the fire became a furnace, and the explosion of fulfilment felt as if it might annihilate her in the white heat of the flames.

A long while—what seemed like a whole lifetime—later, she stirred in the warm circle of his arms, curled against him in a daze of happiness. Luc levered himself up on to one elbow, and turned her face towards him, his eyes very bright beneath heavy, deceptively sleepy lids.

'How do you feel?' he murmured huskily.

'Wonderful!' She blinked and then stared up at him, wide-eyed, hardly daring to believe that the months of guilty denial, the agonising episode in the Caribbean, had resolved so abruptly into such blissful rapport.

'Tell me about your engagement to Edward,' he said slowly, tightening his arm around her when she tensed instinctively. 'No, I am not beginning our feud all over again, *cara*. But...I am puzzled that you never made love.'

'I know...' She felt her tension melting away again. 'I...I just wasn't ready...and, after one fiasco when I panicked, Edward was too *gentlemanly* to push me. It sort of became accepted that we'd wait until we married.'

Luc's expression spoke volumes about his opinion of such gentlemanly behaviour.

'Why didn't you tell me, Verity?' he chided softly. 'I would have taken greater care.'

'Greater care? Do you mean . . . against the possibility of a child?' she queried unsteadily, her heart contracting.

'No,' he teased gently, his eyes darkening with fresh emotion. 'Why should I wish to do that, with the woman I love most in the world?'

A flush of colour crept into her cheeks, and she pressed her hands to her face, suddenly overwhelmed with happiness.

'Do you really mean that?'

'With all my heart . . .' He stood up suddenly, supremely oblivious of his nakedness as he crossed the room and shrugged on a black towelling robe, returning with another in blue silk Paisley for Verity. 'And I brought something for you, from the Villa Laguna. Something you left behind . . .'

He retrieved something from the dressing-table, and handed it to her. The amber pendant gleamed in her fingers, the circle of diamonds burning like white fire in their oval setting.

'Thank you . . . it's so beautiful, Luc.'

He bent to kiss her, and for several minutes further conversation was out of the question. When they finally drew apart, she smiled at him shakily, reaching to fasten the pendant around her neck. Her fingers refused to function, and Luc came to her rescue, lifting her hair and bending his head to kiss the hollow of her throat when he'd secured the catch at her nape, and then sliding his hands down to caress the soft curve of her breasts with possessive, growing urgency. She shivered, catching her breath, twisting her arms around him again, almost aching with the need to get as close to him as possible.

'Luc, about Edward...' she whispered.

'No, let's forget Edward.' Luc's voice held a thicker, huskier note. 'Feeling guilty about Edward has caused us both enough trouble over the last twelve months!'

'But I want to explain,' she insisted shakily. 'I did love him, but not enough. He was undemanding, and safe, and a good friend, and I was very, very fond of him. But when I met you last year, in Florida, it was like...like instant recognition. I knew for the first time what it would feel like to be fathoms deep in love with someone, and I was terrified! And I felt so guilty because my relationship with Edward suddenly seemed so inadequate, and I was mentally being unfaithful to him, and then for those awful few minutes at the club ball that night I was more than that, I was very nearly physically unfaithful to him——'

'What made you so afraid?' Luc cut in softly, pushing the tangled hair from her eyes to inspect her face. 'Why were you so determined to settle for half-measures with Edward, Verity?'

She was silent, struggling to sort out her muddled thoughts. Finally, she said slowly, 'My parents, I suppose...I mean, when they died I was shattered. But then I discovered my father had been seeing another woman. My mother trusted him, adored him...I'd always thought they were totally committed to each other. Finding out that it had all been false...it was like...like a double betrayal. Can you understand? It sounds so silly, but it felt as if, by dying, my parents had deserted me, when I loved them both so much...and then as if my father had deserted my mother, secretly, with all those years of cheating...'

She stopped, floundering, uncertain how to explain, but Luc nodded slowly, reaching to draw her back into his arms.

'I understand, *cara*. I know how it feels to discover that someone you love has cheated you.'

'Juliette?' Verity forced herself to ask the question which frightened her most. 'Do you still love her, Luc?'

'Still?' His reaction was wry. 'I doubt if I ever loved her. Not enough. My feelings for her were calf-love. Immature. They were not strong enough to withstand the deception and betrayal which followed. For years I have felt nothing but pity for Juliette.'

There was a silence, their eyes locked in wordless communication.

'The past is over,' Luc murmured finally, his eyes very intent on hers, 'and so is my involvement with Juliette. I've loved you all these months, Verity. From the first moment we met. Do not doubt that. I have done everything in my power to be sure you wanted for nothing, that you were protected and secure...'

'Showering me with business connections?' she teased softly. 'Playing fairy godfather?'

His mouth twisted in self-derision as he nodded.

'As you say. I have lost more sleep, dreamed more restless dreams, slayed more imaginary dragons on your behalf than I care to admit to, *cara*. So tell me once again—do you love me? I want to hear you say it, now, so I can truly believe it is so.'

'It is so,' she smiled, huskily mocking his deteriorating English. 'It is very much so, Luc!'

'*Ten cuidado*, take care,' he breathed hoarsely. 'Do not mock me, Verity!'

'I love you,' she said simply, her eyes shining as she saw the dark wash of colour across the deep tan of his skin.

'*Bueno*!' There was a flare of fierce, raw triumph in his eyes which made her catch her breath involuntarily. 'Then only one complication remains. How to persuade you to marry me, when my sister and her husband are witnesses to your avowed aversion to weddings?'

'Is that an official proposal?' she queried, her voice slightly unsteady, her expression when she looked up at him so radiant that he closed his eyes for an instant in a gesture of mute relief.

'*Si, cara.*' His slow, devastating smile was transforming his features. 'It is an official proposal! And you will recall that our marriage is inevitable, *no es verdad*? Pre-ordained, written in the stars... or engraved on the palm of your hand? Your "witch" deserves official recognition, don't you think?'

Verity gave a choked laugh, and buried her head against Luc's chest.

'Yes, she does,' she whispered, shivering as he closed his arms around her.

He kissed her, a long, hard, searching kiss which made her head spin and turned her stomach to water.

'I want you to be mine, Verity!' he whispered unevenly, pushing her away again slightly and raking her flushed face with burning, hungry eyes. 'I want you with me always. I will try to make no arrogant demands on you, *cara*... but I confess I don't want to share you with anyone or anything!'

'And my business?' she queried, blinking at the intensity of his gaze.

'As you choose,' he assured her, with a wry, self-mocking twist of his mouth. 'To keep, to sell—it would be your choice!'

Verity felt a smile tugging at the corners of her mouth at the obvious effort it took him to say it.

'Well...I suppose Sara and Connor might just buy me out,' she mused teasingly, choking back a delicious shiver of reaction as Luc's long fingers began a lazily possessive exploration in places which brought a fresh warmth to her face. 'They're madly in love, and he's already in the catering trade, which will leave me a lady of endless leisure, to humbly devote my entire life to your service...*Luc!*' she finished up on a slight, husky gasp as his caresses grew more insistent.

'Then you *will* marry me, Verity?' There was no laughter in Luc's voice now, only a hard, demanding urgency which melted her against him in total surrender.

'Yes, Luc. I will...'

He crushed her to him in a wave of rough triumph.

'And the brainstorm and the amnesia?' he teased raggedly, his lips against her hair.

She lifted her face to his with a smile of such bewitching ardour that his eyes narrowed to a dark glitter of desire.

'I've just had a very...*convenient* attack of both!' she assured him softly.

'You will never regret it, *cara.*'

'I know.'

And the glow in her eyes, as Luc bent his head to kiss her laughing mouth, held a brilliance which could erase every shadow of the past, leaving only the certainty of a magical, enchanted future together.

Next Month's Romances

Each month you can choose from a wide variety of romance with Mills & Boon. Below are the new titles to look out for next month, why not ask either Mills & Boon Reader Service or your Newsagent to reserve you a copy of the titles you want to buy — just tick the titles you would like and either post to Reader Service or take it to any Newsagent and ask them to order your books.

Please save me the following titles:	Please tick	√
RIDE THE STORM	Emma Darcy	
A DAUGHTER'S DILEMMA	Miranda Lee	
PRIVATE LIVES	Carole Mortimer	
THE WAYWARD WIFE	Sally Wentworth	
HAUNTING ALLIANCE	Catherine George	
RECKLESS CRUSADE	Patricia Wilson	
CRY WOLF	Amanda Carpenter	
LOVE IN TORMENT	Natalie Fox	
STRANGER PASSING BY	Lilian Peake	
PRINCE OF DARKNESS	Kate Proctor	
A BRIDE FOR THE TAKING	Sandra Marton	
JOY BRINGER	Lee Wilkinson	
A WOMAN'S LOVE	Grace Green	
DANGEROUS DOWRY	Catherine O'Connor	
WEB OF FATE	Helena Dawson	
A FAMILY AFFAIR	Charlotte Lamb	

If you would like to order these books in addition to your regular subscription from Mills & Boon Reader Service please send £1.70 per title to: Mills & Boon Reader Service, P.O. Box 236, Croydon, Surrey, CR9 3RU, quote your Subscriber No:...
(If applicable) and complete the name and address details below. Alternatively, these books are available from many local Newsagents including W.H.Smith, J.Menzies, Martins and other paperback stockists from 6th November 1992.

Name:...

Address:...

....Post Code:.........................

To Retailer: If you would like to stock M&B books please contact your regular book/magazine wholesaler for details.

You may be mailed with offers from other reputable companies as a result of this application.
If you would rather not take advantage of these opportunities please tick box ☐

WIN A TRIP TO ITALY

Three lucky readers and their partners will spend a romantic weekend in Italy next May. You'll stay in a popular hotel in the centre of Rome, perfectly situated to visit the famous sites by day and enjoy the food and wine of Italy by night. During the weekend we are holding our first International Reader Party, an exciting celebratory event where you can mingle with Mills & Boon fans from all over Europe and meet some of our top authors.

HOW TO ENTER

We'd like to know just how wonderfully romantic your partner is, and how much Mills & Boon means to you.

Firstly, answer the questions below and then fill in our tie-breaker sentence:

1. **Which is Rome's famous ancient ruin?**

   ❏ The Parthenon   ❏ The Colosseum   ❏ The Sphinx

2. **Who is the famous Italian opera singer?**

   ❏ Nana Mouskouri   ❏ Julio Iglesias   ❏ Luciano Pavarotti

3. **Which wine comes from Italy?**

   ❏ Frascati   ❏ Liebfraumilch   ❏ Bordeaux

Tie-Breaker: Well just how romantic is your man? Does he buy you chocolates, send you flowers, take you to romantic candlelit restaurants? Send us a recent snapshot of the two of you (passport size is fine), together with a caption which tells us in no more than 15 words what makes your romantic man so special you'd like to visit Rome with him as the weekend guests of Mills & Boon.

....

....

....

....

In order to find out more about how much Mills & Boon means to you, we'd like you to answer the following questions:

1. How long have you been reading Mills & Boon books?

❑ One year or less   ❑ 2-5 years   ❑ 6-10 years

❑ 10 years or more

2. Which series do you usually read?

❑ Mills & Boon Romances   ❑ Medical Romances   ❑ Best Seller

❑ Temptation   ❑ Duet   ❑ Masquerade

3. How often do you read them?   ❑ 1 a month or less

❑ 2-4 a month   ❑ 5-10 a month   ❑ More than 10 a month

Please complete the details below and send your entry to: Mills & Boon Reader Service, FREEPOST, P.O. Box 236, Croydon, Surrey CR9 9EL, England.

Name: ....

Address: ....

.... Post Code: ....

Are you a Reader Service subscriber?

❑ No ❑ Yes my Subscriber No. is: ....

RULES & CONDITIONS OF ENTRY

BARBARY WHARF

W❮❯RLDWIDE

BRAND NEW MINI SERIES

As you know there are six books in total. Why not reserve your copies and receive two each month from Mills & Boon Reader Service for only £2.99 each, postage and packing FREE, or enclose a cheque for £17.94 made payable to Mills & Boon to receive all six books at once. Either way you will not miss any of these exciting future titles.

To reserve your **BARBARY WHARF** series, simply complete the coupon below and return it to:-
Mills & Boon Reader Service, FREEPOST PO Box 236, Croydon, CR9 9EL.

MINI SERIES

- - - - - - - - - - - - - - - - ✂ - - -

PLEASE TICK ONE BOX ONLY:

☐ **YES!** Please reserve me a subscription to the **BARBARY WHARF** mini series. I understand that you will send me two books each month and invoice me for £5.98.　　EPBW1

☐ **YES!** Please send me all six books in the **BARBARY WHARF** mini series. I enclose a cheque for £17.94. Postage and packing free.　　EPBW2

Ms/Mrs/Miss/Mr _____

Address _____

_____

_____ Postcode _____

Signature _____ Are you a Reader Service Subscriber　Yes ☐　No ☐

Subscription No. _____